"We found a foster family for Lula."

Skye let out a gasp. She appeared to be unsettled by the news.

"Everything is going to move very fast from this point forward," Ryan said. Some instinct told him that Skye needed to prepare herself for Lula's departure.

Skye looked down at the baby. "You hear that, sweetie? It's such good news." The upbeat words coming out of her mouth didn't match her sad expression.

"Well, I've got to help with the arrangements. I'll be in touch shortly." Ryan gave a nod before walking toward his vehicle. There was no point in resurrecting their discussion about her negative feelings toward him. She was going to believe what she wanted. And she believed he'd gotten in the way of her wedding. Bad-mouthed her to Tyler.

Just as he was about to get in the cruiser, Ryan heard Skye calling after him. He turned around as she came rushing toward him, a slightly panicked expression etched on her face. Emotion shimmered in her eyes.

"Please don't send Lula away," Skye beseeched him. "I—I want to be her foster mom."

Belle Calhoune grew up in a small town in Massachusetts. Married to her college sweetheart, she is raising two lovely daughters in Connecticut. A dog lover, she has one mini poodle and a black Lab. Writing for the Love Inspired line is a dream come true. Working at home in her pajamas is one of the best perks of the job. Belle enjoys summers in Cape Cod, traveling and reading.

Visit the Author Profile page at LoveInspired.com.

An Alaskan Blessing

BELLE CALHOUNE

LOVE INSPIRED
INSPIRATIONAL ROMANCE

LOVE INSPIRED®
INSPIRATIONAL ROMANCE

Recycling programs for this product may not exist in your area.

ISBN-13: 978-1-335-93142-9

An Alaskan Blessing

Love Inspired
22 Adelaide St. West, 41st Floor
Toronto, Ontario M5H 4E3, Canada
www.LoveInspired.com

Printed in Lithuania

MIX
Paper | Supporting responsible forestry
FSC® C021394

Blessed are the peacemakers:
for they shall be called the children of God.
—*Matthew* 5:9

To my girls, Amber and Sierra,
for making me a mother.

Acknowledgments

With deep appreciation for the readers
who so enthusiastically support my work.
This wouldn't be possible without you.

For my editor, Katie Gowrie. Looking forward to
brainstorming on many more projects.
I'm thankful for all of your help and enthusiasm.

For my agent, Jessica Alvarez.
Forever grateful for our partnership.

Big thanks to my friend Necee Lomelino,
who assisted me so much with Alaska questions.
Much appreciated. Also to Ruth Lewis, who was
so helpful regarding safe haven/CPS and
law enforcement procedures in Alaska.

And lastly to Alaska Family Services, especially
Karissa, for answering all of my questions.
I'm indebted to you.

Chapter One

A cold Alaskan wind swept over Skye Drummond as she made the trek from the family homestead toward the general store. The Serenity Mountains, blanketed with snow, rose up in the distance. Even though the sun was just rising, and she was normally sleeping at this hour, Skye felt excited about her new role at Sugar Works. For more than a decade her family's business had specialized in birch syrup with low amounts of sugar and additives. With the opening of the shop, Sugar's Place—which had been named for Skye's late mother and which Skye proudly managed—they'd branched out in the last few years to specialty items such as candles, soaps, blankets, clothing and a few food items. Her father was convinced Sugar Works was poised to become a household name in Alaska and the lower forty-eight states. Skye wished she had an ounce of his confidence. It would be nice to walk through life feeling good about herself.

Walking to the shop every morning helped

Skye clear her mind. The last three years had been tough on her. In a perfect world she would be married now and starting a family. But being ditched on the day of her wedding by her ex-fiancé, Tyler Flint, had ended those plans. Her heart still ached every time she thought about it…and him. She wasn't in love with him anymore, but it hurt to know he hadn't found her worthy enough to be his bride.

You have a lot of growing up to do.

Those had been the last words Tyler had said to her before he'd walked out of the church and vanished from her life. Skye shuddered every time she remembered the comment he'd spoken in the church vestibule right before her heart completely shattered. And even though she had tried really hard to move on with her life, it had been extremely difficult, especially in a small town like Serenity Peak. She'd been humiliated by the town gossip, along with the implication that she'd done something so terrible that Tyler had been forced to call things off. The rumor mill had cut her to shreds. As a result, she'd gone inward.

One step at a time. That was what she had been trying to do ever since that terrible day. It hadn't been easy trying to grow from her awful experience and demonstrate that she wasn't unworthy of love. She breathed in the pristine air and reminded herself to stay calm and serene. Letting her emotions get the best of her served absolutely no purpose.

You are a work in progress.
You are worthy.
You are kind.
You are a child of God.

She repeated the affirmations in her head. Little by little she was getting her self-esteem back. Feeling good about herself was one of her biggest goals.

There wasn't an abundance of snow on the ground, but temperatures were frigid.

When she was about ten feet away, Skye noticed a basket sitting on the front porch leading to the general store. She hoped it wasn't anything perishable that had been delivered last night. Sometimes delivery trucks ended up at Sugar's Place instead of the family home down the road.

She suddenly stopped in her tracks. The little noise she'd just heard emanating from the basket sounded like a baby's cry.

She must be hearing things. Why would a baby be out here at such an early hour? Especially without an adult around.

Skye let out a shout as she saw a little arm raised up in the air. She quickened her pace and vaulted up the steps, peering down into the face of the most adorable infant she'd ever seen.

"Oh, sweet baby, you must be freezing." Skye didn't waste another moment before she scooped up the basket and placed it on her hip, then rushed to unlock the front door. Once she stepped inside, heat suffused her. She was grateful for the warmth in the store. This child needed to be warmed up immediately.

Skye rested the basket on a nearby counter and placed her palm on the baby's cheek, which was only slightly cool.

"Hmm, you don't seem too cold, but I have no idea how long you were out in the elements. I'm no doctor, but wee little ones aren't supposed to be left out in the Alaskan cold." She bit her lip. Skye had no idea what to do. She felt like pinching herself. Was this really happening? An actual baby had been left at the shop.

Skye looked the infant over. Judging by her pink blanket, the baby was a little girl. Skye had an urge to cuddle her and tell her everything would be all right. *Who would leave a baby on the doorstep of the family store?* She needed to call the authorities immediately.

Skye reached for her cell phone and dialed the state trooper's office. When the receptionist, Karissa Daniels, answered the phone, a feeling of panic rose inside of her. She needed help! This wasn't something she could deal with on her own. She began to explain at a fast pace. "Slow down, Skye," Karissa said. "I can't understand what you're saying."

She reminded herself to stay calm. *Dear Lord, help me. For whatever reason You placed this child in my path and under my protection.*

"Someone left a baby at the shop's front door," Skye repeated slowly. "I need a state trooper to come here to check out the situation. I'm not sure what to do," she admitted.

"I'll send someone over right away. Have you reached out to Poppy?" Karissa asked. Poppy Matthews was a local doctor and one of Skye's closest friends. "She might need to check the infant out."

"Yes, I will," Skye promised before concluding the call. She didn't think the baby had been harmed by exposure to the elements, but she wasn't certain. It was best to have a medical expert make that determination. Skye called Doc Poppy at her medical clinic, and Poppy promised to head over to Sugar's Place as soon as she finished up with a patient. She quickly dialed her father, then Violet, her older sister. Both calls went straight to their voice mails. Skye had a feeling neither one had cell phone service. It was an odd problem they had from time to time in certain areas on their property.

Ten minutes later a vehicle marked State Trooper pulled up in front of the shop. Skye had been standing by the window, eagerly awaiting their arrival. The baby had slept peacefully, which astounded Skye. She had been watching carefully for the slightest sign that something was wrong. Not that she was an expert on infants, but she'd helped Violet when Chase was a baby.

Skye drew in a sharp breath when she spotted the handsome state trooper stepping out of his patrol car. Ryan Campbell. With his dark hair and blue eyes, he was extremely easy on the eyes. He seemed very well aware of his appeal, which annoyed her to no end. She'd known him since they were babies, yet lately she'd felt as if she didn't know him at all. He was Tyler's close friend. Skye always had the feeling he was being judgmental toward her. And finding her to be lacking in every way imaginable.

He was the very last person she wanted to deal with right now, although she couldn't afford to be picky. This sweet baby girl needed all of their help, even if it meant dealing with her ex-fiancé's best friend.

Ryan Campbell walked toward Sugar's Place, his mind racing with the details of the call he'd just received from dispatch. An abandoned baby had been found by Skye Drummond at her family's general store! Of all the calls in the world, why had he been given this particular one? Not only was the incident highly unusual, but the call had been made from someone who disliked him. Skye was always icy toward him now. Because he'd been best buddies with Tyler back then, she'd decided to lump him into the same category as the man who'd subjected her to public humiliation and broken her heart. On the rare occasions when they'd crossed paths over the past few years, Skye had given him nothing more than a cold look.

He'd gotten the message, loud and clear from Skye. They were no longer friends. It had been a long time since they'd been close confidants— Ryan knew he'd alienated her during his rabble-rousing phase in his early twenties—but it still hurt that she couldn't even seem to look him in the eye now.

He inhaled a deep breath before he turned the knob and stepped inside. As usual, the sight of the stunning blonde caused him to lose his equilibrium a little bit. Skye had always been the most beautiful girl in Serenity Peak, with charm and wit in addition to her striking looks. For as long as he could remember, Skye had been Tyler's girl, until he'd called off their wedding.

"Good morning, Skye," Ryan said, taking off his hat and holding it against his chest. It was uncanny how nervous he always felt in this woman's presence. Her sea blue eyes always seemed to cut straight through him like lasers.

"Hello," Skye said curtly, bobbing her head in his direction. "The baby's right here." She reached out and patted the side of the baby carrier. Her movements were gentle and graceful. Ryan sensed she didn't want a single thing to disturb the precious bundle.

Ryan took a few strides in Skye's direction, quickly closing the space between them. He looked down at the baby adorned in various shades of pink. With wispy brown hair poking out from her cap and full cheeks, she was lovely. Her eyes were pressed closed and she was sleeping peacefully.

"She fell asleep shortly after I discovered her," Skye said. "Hasn't even made a peep since I brought her inside. Despite everything, she seems to be pretty content."

Ryan thought it was amazing, under the circumstances, that the baby remained in a tranquil state. "Do you have any idea who she belongs to?" he asked.

Skye's blue eyes widened. "No. None at all. I'm not even sure how old she is. I can't understand why anyone left her here of all places." She shuddered. "I don't want to think about what could have happened if I'd overslept or dawdled over breakfast. When I found her she was cool to the touch but just barely. And she wasn't in any distress."

Winter in Alaska was fairly brutal and the last time he'd checked, this morning's temps were hovering around fifteen degrees.

"It's just a hunch, but I think someone placed her on the porch just as you got close to the shop. Otherwise, she would have been frozen."

"If so, then someone planned this out," Skye murmured.

"Looks like there's something tucked into the side of the carrier." Ryan reached down and lightly tugged at the object. He pulled out a piece of paper and unfolded the white stationery. A single word stared back at him. *Lula.*

"What does it say?" Skye asked, leaning toward him.

He held the scrap of paper up for her to see. "Lula. That must be her name."

"Lula," Skye repeated, a soft smile tugging at the corners of her mouth before it stretched out across her entire face. "What a sweet name."

He hadn't seen Skye smile much since Tyler broke her heart. He'd almost forgotten how radiant she looked when she was happy. Who would have thought that an itty-bitty baby would spark such joy in Skye?

"It's a good name," Ryan said. "And from what I can see, she was well taken care of." He ran his hand alongside the baby carrier. "This is a solid product. And the blanket and clothes are made from fine materials. This baby was loved."

"You can tell all that from her clothes and the carrier?" Skye asked with a frown.

"It's a feeling," Ryan said, "based on what I've observed. In a situation like this one, it's important to absorb the clues. They can tell us a lot."

"Well, if she was so loved, why was she abandoned?" Skye scoffed. "Who would do such a thing?" Her voice quivered with anger.

Ryan locked gazes with her. He counted to ten in his head before responding. "Perhaps someone who was overwhelmed or desperate. It's not my place to judge. My main priority is the baby and making sure she's okay."

Skye bristled. "Of course. Same here. That's why I contacted your office. An innocent baby is at stake." She moved closer to the carrier and placed her hand protectively on the side.

"You did a good thing, Skye, but I can take it from here," he told her in a gentle voice, sensing she needed reassurance. Immediately her shoulders relaxed as she stared down at the peaceful infant.

"What happens now?" she asked, her eyes wide with interest.

Ryan drew his brows together. "That all depends on whether we can locate the parents or not. Until we can figure things out, this little lady is going into foster care." Just saying the words out loud caused a little hitch in his heart.

Skye let out a gasp and raised her hand to her throat. "I know that's the normal protocol, but isn't there anything else to be done until the parents are tracked down?" She seemed to hesitate momentarily. "My father is in the system as a foster parent although he may not have his current certification." She bit her lip. "It's been a while since my family fostered."

"The certification would have to be current." Ryan ran his hand over his face. The situation was complex. That was for certain. "This is new territory for us. It isn't every day a baby is dropped off at someone's place of business. And honestly, the parents might not be in a position to raise her. Clearly whoever left her was in distress of some sort."

All of a sudden the door flew open to reveal Skye's father, Abel Drummond, striding into the store. With his long grizzled beard and broad shoulders, he always made quite an impression. "Skye! What's going on? That message you left didn't make any sense. I thought you said something about a ba—" Abel halted in his tracks as soon as he spotted the baby carrier. He let out a low whistle. "A baby?" If the situation hadn't been so serious, Ryan might have chuckled at the dumbfounded expression etched on Abel's face.

"Morning, Abel," Ryan greeted him.

Abel's mouth hung open as he rushed to his daughter's side. "A baby?"

"Yes, Daddy," Skye said somberly. "I found her on the porch." Skye quickly brought her father up to speed, barely stopping to catch her breath.

Abel ran a shaky hand over his face. "Never thought I'd see this twice in one lifetime." His words came out in a rasp as a stunned expression crept across his face.

"Twice?" Ryan asked. "Has this happened before?"

Abel nodded. "Years ago, when my wife was still with us, we fostered a baby that had been left at the homestead. Skye was barely out of middle school at the time."

"What happened?" Ryan asked. The story sounded vaguely familiar, but he was filled with curiosity about the specific details.

"We became a foster family," Skye said, smiling at her dad. "Little Danny was a sweetheart and a blessing for all of us. I finally knew what it felt like to be a big sister."

A wistful look emanated from Abel's eyes. "He stayed with us for six months. Then he was adopted by his forever family," Abel said. "We still get Christmas cards from the Johnsons every year, updating us on his life. They live over in Kodiak."

Ryan couldn't help but wonder if the two incidents were related in any way. What were the odds of this happening twice to one family? He frowned. Was a clue to this baby's identity in the Drummond family's past?

"What's that look for?" Skye asked. "Are we suspects?" She seemed to aim for levity, but he sensed the steely edge to her tone.

"Skye," Abel said in a warning tone.

Clearly it hadn't taken long for Skye's coldness toward him to rise to the surface. He shouldn't let it bother him, but it rankled a bit. Why was he the focus of her anger instead of her ex-fiancé? The last time he checked, he hadn't been the one to leave her at the altar. Guilt by association, he imagined.

Ryan reminded himself to go easy on her. She was still nursing a world of hurt. "I'm here in a professional capacity, Skye. Of course you're not implicated in anything, but I need to keep my mind open to any and all connections that might result in any leads. It's important that we locate Lula's parents."

"We appreciate you coming out here, Ryan," Abel said. "There's nothing more treasured in this world than a child." He slid his arm around Skye's waist and pulled her close to his side.

Abel's words resonated with him. Ryan knew that as a single father who'd raised two daughters after his wife's untimely death, children meant the world to Abel.

"I couldn't agree more," Ryan said. "I fully intend to keep her safe while she's in my care."

"Where will you take her?" Skye asked, lips trembling. Raw emotion emanated from her face. For a moment he thought she might burst into tears.

The question stumped Ryan. He didn't know the protocol for abandoned babies. There were a few families in town who fostered kids, but he wasn't certain about their current status in the program. One woman, Dora Pryor, was getting on in years and not in good health. He would definitely need to contact his boss, Gideon Ross, to find out how to proceed. Finding a suitable foster family in a town as small as Serenity Peak might be tricky. According to Skye, her father hadn't fostered in a while and his certification might not be current. Plus, he was a full-time business owner of Sugar Works. If Abel hadn't mentioned fostering this baby, it wasn't Ryan's place to make the suggestion.

He scratched his jaw and did his best to avoid looking into Skye's azure blue eyes. Ryan didn't want to risk reigniting the feelings he'd once harbored for her. Once she and Tyler had started dating, he'd put those feelings to rest, but he didn't want to take any chances. Skye Drummond was the type of woman who might cause a person to forget their very own name.

"Honestly, I'm not sure. I need to talk to Gideon," he admitted. "And locate some potential foster families." He stopped short of saying that he might have to fly the baby out of Serenity Peak to a place with more fostering opportunities. Judging by the way that Skye was standing so close to the baby carrier, she was feeling protective.

"Poppy is on her way over to examine Lula. Maybe we should just wait a bit and let her check the baby out before any decisions are made," Skye said.

"That sounds reasonable to me," Abel said with a nod. "Her health is of the utmost importance, especially since she was found out in the elements."

Good points, especially since he wasn't certain about his next steps. In that the Drummonds had served as a foster family in the past, he felt confident about leaving Lula with them while he sorted things out.

"Will you be all right with the baby if I head back to the office for a little bit?" Ryan asked. He planned to radio Gideon and explain the situation once he got back to the car. By the time he arrived back at the state trooper's office, maybe his boss would have a plan of action.

"We'll be fine," Abel said. "I can run into town for diapers and formula."

"Yes, Daddy. It would be great to have a bottle ready for her when she wakes up, which could be at any moment," Skye said, biting her lip.

"I'll be back as soon as I can," Ryan said with a curt nod. Something told him that Skye wouldn't care if he ever returned at all. She simply stared at him without making a single comment.

He made his way back to his vehicle and sat there a short while, mulling over the stunning turn of events. His morning had started off with quite a bang, and today's events left no doubt that he had chosen the right path. Becoming a state trooper had been Ryan's way of turning his life around. Instead of running wild all over Serenity Peak as he'd done in his bad-boy phase, he was now helping people and doing his best to make a difference.

Still, the incident had brought Skye Drummond back into his orbit. Honestly, he wasn't sure which was more startling. Dealing with an abandoned baby or having to stand face-to-face with a woman who wanted nothing to do with him.

Chapter Two

Skye looked out the window as Ryan drove away from Sugar's Place. She'd watched him walk around the perimeter of the general store before getting on his radio and having a conversation with someone. Moments later he sped off. Senior Trooper Gideon was on the other end of the line, she imagined. He was the most respected man in Serenity Peak, with her own father running a close second. She had never been more relieved to see the back of someone as when Ryan headed out the door.

"I'm glad *he's* gone," she said, turning back toward her father.

Abel let out a sigh. "You need to take it easy on him, Skye. Ryan's a good man."

"I used to think so," Skye acknowledged. "But then I remember that if it wasn't for him, I might be married right now." The words slipped out of her mouth before she could rein them in.

Her dad made a tutting sound. "That's neither here nor there. Can you honestly say you'd want to be Tyler's wife after how he treated you? And frankly, I think it was pretty cowardly of your ex to try to hide behind his friend's opinion of you. If that was even the truth."

She's not ready for marriage. The words were burned in Skye's memory like a permanent tattoo. How dare Ryan have uttered those words about her to her fiancé mere hours before they were scheduled to walk down the aisle? Ever since then Skye had felt unworthy of love. Of course it was Tyler's fault for breaking things off with her at the altar, but why had Ryan badmouthed her to her fiancé? He had placed so much doubt in Tyler's mind about walking down the aisle that he'd bailed at the last minute.

She folded her arms around her middle. "At that point Tyler had no reason to lie. He'd already called things off," she said, her voice wavering as the hurtful memories crashed over her. She had fallen out of love with Tyler ages ago, but she was still living with the fallout from the wedding that wasn't. All of her hopes and dreams had crashed and burned in that one horrific moment. She'd spent the last few years picking up the pieces. And Ryan, her childhood friend, had played a role in her downfall.

Abel shook his head. "You're still seeing things through a cloudy lens. I pray that you get clarity, because that's a huge step toward complete healing. Tyler broke your heart, not Ryan."

But hadn't Ryan broken her heart too? She'd once considered him a friend. Abel held up his keys. "I'm heading off to town. I'll be back as quick as I can."

Before she could even respond, he'd rushed out the door. Skye hated her father being disappointed in her outlook. Ever since she was a little girl, she'd sought to make her parents proud of her. She wished she'd done something worthwhile in her life to warrant it, but Skye knew her main claim to fame had always been her looks. For many years she'd been delighted to be known as the most beautiful girl in town, but lately all it did was make her feel empty inside. She yearned to make a difference, to do something of value. But she still felt as if she was merely treading water.

Seeing Ryan had served as a trigger for her emotions, and she hadn't been able to keep a lid on them. She had stuffed her feelings down into this little black hole, but they had risen to the surface as soon as Ryan pulled up in his department-issue vehicle. For so long she'd managed to avoid running into him, but her good fortune had run out this morning. How many times had she imagined confronting him about what Tyler had revealed the morning of their wedding? So far she had avoided a face-to-face encounter with her old friend, but she yearned to tell him how she felt about his comments.

Tyler broke your heart, not Ryan. Her father was right. Maybe the truth was that Ryan's actions had been so out of character while a part of her had always known who Tyler was. Back in the day Ryan had been the one she'd confided in and shared all her dreams for the future with, due to their close bond. It hurt to think that none of it had meant anything at all to him.

A few minutes after her father's departure, the sound of tires crunching on the snow drew Skye's attention back to the window. She watched as Poppy stepped down from her tomato red truck with her black medical kit in hand. With her flawless brown skin and long, flowing braids, Doc Poppy was a stunning woman.

Skye strode to the door and flung it open, relief flowing through her at the sight of her friend. "Poppy! I don't think I've ever been so happy to see anyone in my life." The doctor's presence was incredibly reassuring in this tense situation.

As she entered the shop, Poppy paused to give Skye a hug. Skye admired her friend so much. Poppy was a brilliant woman who'd devoted her life to serving the medical needs of the Serenity Peak community. She had a purpose and a mission—to heal and to educate.

"Where is my little patient? Ever since you called, my curiosity has been off the charts," Poppy said, her brown eyes twinkling.

"She's right over here," Skye said, beckoning Poppy to follow her, "and according to the note in her carrier, her name is Lula." Skye spoke in a whisper and placed a finger on her mouth. "Believe it or not, she's stayed asleep this entire time."

Poppy looked down at Lula and smiled. "She's a beauty. I hate to tell you, but she's probably going to wake up as soon as I start the exam."

Skye made a face. "Let's just hope she's not too hungry. My dad went into town for supplies."

"Good thing I brought some formula and diapers," Poppy said with a wink. "Just in case."

Skye let out a relieved breath. "You are literally the best," she crowed, squeezing her friend's hand. "This town is fortunate to have you."

Poppy had only been in Serenity Peak for a few years, yet she had made incredible contributions to the local community.

"You're going to give me a swollen head." Poppy chuckled. "Okay, Skye, if you can grab a blanket I can place her down on this sofa and do the exam," she suggested.

"Sure thing," Skye said, going behind the counter and reaching for a plush blanket. She handed it over to Poppy, who plucked Lula from her carrier and placed her down on her back. Seconds later Lula's face twisted and she opened her mouth to let out a cry. Her lids fluttered open, revealing a pair of beautiful, piercing blue eyes.

"This won't take long, Lula," Poppy crooned as she began undressing her. "Might as well give you a diaper change while I'm at it." She turned toward Skye. "Can you hand me the bag? I had to guess on the sizes."

Skye grabbed the bag and reached inside for the formula and a bottle. "Why don't I go heat a bottle up while you check her out?"

"Sounds like a plan," Poppy said with a nod as she focused on the baby. Lula's cries were beginning to escalate, which caused Skye to move a little faster as she made her way to the small kitchen in the back of the store.

A few minutes later Skye returned with a warmed-up bottle. "Something tells me she's ready for a feeding," Poppy said. Lula looked at Skye with big, tear-filled eyes as Poppy handed her over.

Thankfully she'd had plenty of practice with babies during her teen years with her nephew, Chase, who was now nine years old. As soon as Skye placed the bottle near Lula's lips and cradled her against her, she began to drink with gusto. Skye began to hum to Lula in a soothing manner. The baby felt so solid in her arms, as if she was meant to be there.

"She appears to be in perfect shape," Poppy said. "I'm estimating she's four to five months old and a very healthy weight. She's not showing any signs of malnutrition." Poppy knit her brows together. "In fact, I would say she was very well taken care of. My gut is telling me she was well loved, although I know that's not very scientific."

"I know exactly what you mean." Poppy had just confirmed her growing suspicions. At first she had been skeptical of Ryan's comment earlier, based on the fact that the child had been abandoned, but Skye had been making assumptions. "Which makes it even more perplexing that she was left on our doorstep."

"Not really. Sometimes parents make hard choices if they don't think they can raise a baby. And those reasons can be complicated. Finances. Age. Mental outlook. Not being in a stable relationship." Poppy sent her a pointed look. "Trust me, I've seen it all during my years in practice."

The door crashed open and her father came barreling through, his face as red as a berry. He held up a large brown paper bag. "I've got the supplies."

His gaze went straight to Lula lying in Skye's arms. "Oh," he said. "Looks like she's all set." A tinge of disappointment was laced in his voice.

Bless his heart. Her father always did everything he could to help others without fail. Now was no exception. "Poppy brought reinforcements, but don't worry, those won't go to waste," Skye explained.

"Right," he said with a smile. "We can always hand them over to Ryan when he takes her to the foster family."

Just hearing those words from her father's mouth caused Skye to clutch Lula closer against her chest. What would happen to her once Ryan returned? Who would she end up with? And why had Lula's parents left her at Sugar's Place?

Lord, please watch over this precious little girl. Keep her safe and protected, now and always.

An hour later, Ryan was heading back to Sugar's Place, with Gideon following closely behind him in his own vehicle. Once he'd told his boss about Lula, Gideon had been eager to see things for himself out at the property. Ryan was grateful that Gideon would help explain the situation to the Drummonds. Although he loved being a state trooper, Ryan was still getting a feel for the position. Having Gideon as a mentor was invaluable. He was always cool under pressure and there was no way in creation that Skye would intimidate him.

The moment they stepped back inside the shop,

Ryan's gaze went straight to Skye. She was now sitting in a rocking chair, holding Lula and singing to her in a sweet voice. Despite the uncertainty of the situation, Skye projected an air of grace and calm. He tried not to stare, but it was difficult to look away from the sight of the two of them.

He had no idea how the Drummonds would react to his update. All he could do was pray it would all work out in the best interest of Lula. Every child deserved a home, safety and a family to call their own.

Gideon clapped Abel on the shoulder. "Hey, there, Abel," he greeted him. He smiled over at Skye, nodding at her.

"Hey, Gideon," Skye said, gifting the senior trooper with a radiant smile. Ryan, on the other hand, received nothing more than a blank stare.

Ryan let out a sigh of frustration. At some point he needed to ask Skye why she was treating him like public enemy number one. He seemed to get more heat than Tyler, whom he never saw anymore. Was there something he didn't know? Some specific reason she was being so salty toward him?

"Ryan got me up to speed on the baby," Gideon said. "We're going to do everything we can to find out who the parents are." Gideon's voice radiated with confidence.

"In the meantime, Lula's welfare is of the utmost importance," Ryan stressed.

"For all of us," Abel said with a nod. "We need to protect her at all costs."

"Doc Poppy was just here examining her. She told us Lula is in wonderful shape," Skye explained. "It's a tremendous blessing to know she's healthy."

"That's good news. She just spoke to Gideon a little while ago and let him know she's medically cleared," Ryan said. "It's one less thing we have to worry about." He'd thought of nothing else on the way back over to Sugar Works, the family business located on the Drummond's sprawling property. Ryan had offered up numerous prayers on Lula's behalf. There was something about the little girl and the circumstances of her being dropped off at the gift shop that tugged at his heartstrings. Gideon always warned him not to let his emotions guide him when he was working a case. He needed to focus on facts.

Ryan cleared his throat. He locked gazes with Skye. "At the moment, we need to find a foster family for Lula. Gideon and I both made a few calls that led to dead ends."

"What are you saying?" Skye asked. "Where will she go?"

"We don't have a family to take her in right now, which means we're going to have to fly her to another town that has foster care openings," Gideon explained.

"Problem is, we don't have that sorted out yet," Ryan added. "Which is why we're wondering if Lula can stay with your family for a few days. I checked into it and Abel's certification is still current. Since you're in the system as a foster family we won't be breaking any rules." Ryan held his breath as he awaited their reaction. This was no easy ask, but there weren't a lot of options. He knew the Drummonds were bighearted folks who cared deeply about their community.

Abel let out a shocked sound. Skye looked over at her father with a pleading expression. "If it were up to me I'd say yes," she blurted out. "Daddy? What do you think?"

Abel ran a hand over his face. "Skye, we're not equipped to take care of a baby."

"What do we really need that we don't already have or can't figure out?" Skye asked. Lula stopped drinking from the bottle and peered up at Skye as if she knew something of great importance was being discussed. "Violet has all of Chase's baby stuff up in the attic. You know she couldn't bear to give away anything, so it's all there."

Abel reached out and patted Skye on the shoulder. "But we have so much work to do here.

We're at the season when the sap is most plentiful. I'm not sure we can swing it."

"But I'm working here at the shop for the most part. I can ask Kira if she wants to pick up some more hours," Skye pressed. She stood up and began swaying from side to side with Lula in her arms. "It's not like we haven't done this before."

Ryan felt a burst of sympathy for Abel. His daughter wasn't going to make this easy for him. Skye had a reputation for having her father wrapped tightly around her little finger.

A pensive expression settled on Abel's face. "I suppose we could do it for a few days," he conceded.

Skye's smile stretched from ear to ear. She was beaming. "But Jesus said, 'Suffer little children, and forbid them not, to come unto me: for of such is the kingdom of heaven.'"

"Amen," Abel said, reaching out and grazing his knuckles across the baby's cheek.

"Wonderful. I'm going to head out," Gideon said, turning toward Ryan. "I'll leave you to it, then."

"I'll walk you out," Abel said. "There's something I want to pick your brain about."

The two men walked in lockstep toward the door, engrossed in conversation. A silence stretched out between him and Skye, with only the sounds of Lula's gurgles ringing out once she'd finished feeding. For someone whose entire life had been turned upside down today, Lula sure seemed content.

Just then a customer walked through the doors. Skye warmly greeted her. "Hi there, Alyssa. Nice to see you." She turned toward him. "Could you hold Lula while I take care of a little business?"

"Um, sure," Ryan said, hesitating for a moment before holding out his arms so Skye could hand over the baby. It had been a while since he'd held an infant. His uncle Judah had a baby boy, River, but Ryan always shied away from holding him out of fear he might drop him. Maybe it was like riding a bicycle. A person didn't forget how to do certain things, right?

Once Lula was in his arms, Ryan anchored her securely against his chest. He didn't want there to be any chance of her slipping out of his arms. He couldn't believe how solid she felt despite being so small.

"Are you okay?" Skye asked. Her brows were knitted together. It wasn't hard to tell she was concerned about his baby-holding skills.

"We're fine," he said. "Go see to Alyssa."

Skye walked toward her customer after giving him one last probing look.

And then it was just the two of them. Ryan looked down at the baby. She was gazing up at him with wide eyes framed by wispy lashes. She looked so serene.

"Aren't you sweet? I see you're wide-awake now, huh. You look pretty content as far as I can tell." He dipped his head down, placing a hand over her, and whispered, "I'm going to tell you a secret. You're strong, even though you're a wee little thing. And you're going to get stronger every day."

Lula squeezed his finger and let out another gurgling sound. Ryan's heart constricted. He had the strangest feeling she was trying to talk to him. This little girl was a charmer. He couldn't explain how she'd gotten under his skin so quickly, but she brought out tender feelings in him. He wanted to protect her from all the bad things in the world. The thought came out of nowhere, shocking him to his core.

There was no point in getting attached. Lula wasn't going to remain in Serenity Peak for much longer. Ryan wasn't going to be her protector. Matter of fact, their paths probably wouldn't ever cross again. Hopefully, this little girl would find her forever family. In the meantime he was going to look into the identity of Lula's mother in the hopes of tracking her down.

Ryan found himself humming as he walked over to the window and looked out across the Drummonds' massive property. All he could see was the purest white snow, birch trees and the Drummond family home. It made him very curious about the person or persons who had dropped Lula off here at the general store. Down the road there was more activity with the Sugar Works employees and the company trucks. Ryan figured that with all the morning comings and goings at Sugar Works, Lula's folks had gone unnoticed.

"I'll take her now," Skye said, holding out her arms. Ryan moved close to her and slowly began the transfer from his arms to hers. He tried not to notice Skye's long dark lashes or the graceful slope of her neck. A sweet perfumed scent hung over her like a cloud.

"You're a natural," he said, noticing how easily she appeared to be dealing with the unexpected arrival.

"There's nothing more centering than a baby in your midst," Skye said. "And being in a family that fostered really taught me a lot about caring for infants. I always dreamed of fostering a baby myself when I became an adult. Some of the best moments in my life happened when Chase was little."

Thoughts of his cousin Zane swept over him. Zane and Chase had been best buddies. A huge feeling of loss caught him off guard. Ryan was discovering that grief was unpredictable. It rose up out of nowhere and knocked a person off-balance. Zane, along with his mother, Mary, had been killed in a terrible car accident a few years ago. Ryan couldn't put into words how awful it had been for his uncle Judah and the rest of the family. He missed his little buddy, the young cousin who'd always had a case of hero worship when it came to Ryan.

"I grew up taking care of Zane, so I get it," he said, speaking past the lump in his throat. Although he knew that it was important to talk about Zane to keep his memory alive, Ryan struggled to do so without getting emotional. Since he was at Sugar's Place on official business, it wasn't the time or the place. It suddenly hit him that baby River on some level reminded him of Zane. No wonder he hadn't held River yet. Ryan had been worried that his new baby cousin would bring back painful memories. Yet, he'd been fine holding Lula, he reminded himself.

Compassion flared in Skye's eyes. "Zane was such a sweetheart. I know Chase misses him a lot."

Ryan nodded. "We all do," he admitted.

Silence settled over them, with only the sound of Lula's coos ringing out.

"I'm going to head out," he said. "I'll be back day after tomorrow. It's possible I'll be taking the baby to her foster family if we can locate one." He quirked his mouth. "Hopefully we'll get a lead on the parents by then."

Skye's mouth hung open, forming the letter O. "Would they have rights to her? After how they just left her?"

Ryan could tell Skye was still mulling everything over in her mind about Lula's parents and trying to figure out why they'd made such a drastic decision.

"Possibly, depending on the circumstances," Ryan answered. "I don't want to speculate since it's not my area of expertise, but when lawyers and courts get involved, anything's possible."

As Ryan said his goodbyes and left the shop, he cast one last look over his shoulder. Skye was jiggling Lula on her hip and laughing. The duo made a beautiful picture. Skye had matured in the last three years, he realized. He would never have pegged her for the maternal type, although perhaps he'd allowed Tyler's opinions about Skye to influence him. Ryan would never tell Skye, but his former friend had made several comments about her during the course of their relationship that were far from flattering. He was happy to have distanced himself from Tyler's negative energy.

As soon as Ryan got into his vehicle, he reached into his glove compartment and took out the plastic evidence bag he'd placed in there. Earlier this morning he'd inspected the perimeter of Sugar's Place for any clues regarding the baby. Just as he had been on the verge of giving up, he'd spotted a brass button lying in the snow a few feet from the shop's steps. So far it was the only lead they had, even though he couldn't be 100 percent certain it was related to Lula. He would need to ask Skye if it belonged to her or Violet. But there was something about the button that was familiar to him.

Chapter Three

The sound of the front door closing, followed by the tread of boots on the hardwood floor, alerted Skye to someone's arrival at the house. She imagined it was Violet returning from dropping Chase off at school in town.

"Good morning."

Skye turned at the sound of her sister's voice. Violet was dressed for birch syrup tapping in a thick parka, a warm pair of cords and sturdy winter boots. With her strawberry blond hair and freckles, Violet looked like the spitting image of their mother.

"Morning, Violet."

"How'd it go last night?" her sister asked as she walked into the kitchen.

Skye wasn't sure how to answer the question. If she was being completely honest, Lula had been quite a handful. She knew there were shadows resting under her eyes after a night spent trying to soothe the baby. Even though it had been challenging, Skye thought back to her mother doing the same routine with baby Danny. Her parents' devotion had been inspiring. Even in her younger years Skye had aspired to foster a child.

"I'm in dire need of coffee," Skye said with a groan. "Lula is a sweetheart, but she only slept a little bit last night." She jerked her chin in the direction of the baby sleeping peacefully in her carrier. "Which explains why she's fast asleep at the moment."

Violet moved closer and peered down at Lula. She chuckled. "You might need a nap yourself."

Skye let out a throaty laugh. "If I close my eyes I might not wake up until tomorrow. Do you have ten minutes to spare?" She asked, folding her hands in a prayerful manner. "I'd love to take a quick shower before I run into town."

"I could never say no to watching this little lady," Violet said with a grin. "We'll be fine." She shooed Skye away with her hands.

Fifteen minutes later, Skye was feeling invigorated, having cleaned up and dressed in a fresh set of clothes. As she headed back downstairs, she made a mental list of items she needed to pick up in town. Lula wouldn't be staying with her for long, but Skye wanted her to be comfortable. At the top of her list were a few new outfits for the baby.

"Thanks, sis. I feel like a new woman," Skye said as she joined Violet.

"That's all the thanks I need. I'm glad I could help out, but I wish there was more I could do." Violet sounded regretful. "Work is so hectic right now."

"Just being here for me is important," Skye replied, leaning in for a hug. "Your motherhood experiences are worth their weight in gold."

Violet smiled. "Well, I've got to get back to the grind," she said. "What are you up to today?"

"Kira's manning the shop for me, so I'm going to run a few errands in town and bring my little sidekick with me." Skye knew she was grinning from ear to ear. She loved the idea of spending the day with Lula. "Thanks for taking out your car seat from the attic."

"No problem. It's great to put all of Chase's baby stuff to use." She bit her lip. "You're going to get a lot of questions about Lula," Violet said with a raised brow. "Not that you can't handle it, but just beware."

"You're right." Skye shrugged. "I won't go into any of the details, but I'll just say we're helping out as a foster family."

"Good idea," Violet said with a nod. "Especially since Ryan and Gideon are still trying to figure out who she belongs to. No sense in the whole town speculating."

"Not sure I can stop that from happening, but they won't hear it from my lips," Skye said. And she meant it. She hadn't even told her best friend, Molly, about Lula.

Skye headed out of the house at the same time as Violet. She'd bundled Lula in the car seat, covering her with a thick baby blanket to protect her from the cold. Even though Lula was facing in the opposite direction in her car seat, Skye kept looking in the rearview mirror to check on her.

It felt strange to admit, but she was already feeling an attachment to Lula, which didn't make any sense at all. The baby had only been in her life for a little more than twenty-four hours.

Don't get too attached, she reminded herself. Lula would be leaving Serenity Peak as soon as Ryan located a foster family. Skye's gut twisted at the idea of never seeing her again. Her emotions were all over the place and she wasn't sure why. Perhaps caring for Lula reminded her of her own mother's nurturing presence and the gaping hole in her heart that came from losing her.

"It's for the best," she said out loud. What could be better than for Lula to have a safe, secure home with loving caretakers? She would be protected and loved.

I could give her that. The random thought flashed through her mind. Just as quickly she tucked it away, startled by the turn her thoughts had taken. Maybe her lack of sleep was affecting her thinking.

As soon as she reached town, Skye headed toward Main Street, where all the shops and the public library were located. She parked her vehicle, then transferred Lula's carrier into Chase's old stroller. She tested it to make sure it was securely in place before she began walking toward her destination, a children's clothing store. Along the way she exchanged greetings with the townsfolk, many of whom cast curious glances at the stroller. Skye didn't linger so as to avoid any questions.

After half an hour of perusing the racks in the shop, Skye left with several new outfits for Lula. Just looking at the tiny clothing caused a groundswell of emotion to rise up inside of her. Babies outgrew clothes so fast. It would only be a matter of weeks until Lula went up a size. Skye blinked away the moisture welling up in her eyes.

Lord, please protect her. No matter where she goes in this world, watch over my sweet Lula.

Still in need of coffee, Skye headed in the direction of Humbled, a coffeehouse-bookstore on Fifth Street owned by her best friend Molly's family. The moment she stepped inside pushing the stroller, all eyes turned toward her and Lula.

Skye smiled and nodded as she walked toward the counter.

The ambience of the coffee shop was intimate and cozy. The walls were decorated with Bible quotes along with magnificent pictures of the Alaskan landscape. There was a comfortable seating area filled with couches, love seats and intimate tables. The walls were a tranquil egg-shell color. The vibe inside was soothing and peaceful, which was why Skye loved frequenting the establishment. Humbled was her favorite spot in town to browse books, grab a specialty drink and relax. Sometimes she would just sit at a window seat and people-watch.

"Skye!" Molly called out as soon as she spotted her. Molly had been her best friend since the second grade. With full cheeks, freckles and her signature French braids, Molly looked younger than her actual age. She was wholesome and kind. She'd given Skye nothing but loyalty and support throughout the years, and she'd worked so hard building up the bookstore-café until it was a Serenity Peak main attraction.

Molly rounded the counter and gave Skye an enthusiastic hug. "I've been wondering when you would stop by."

"Hey, Molly. It's good to see you," Skye said. Her work at the family business kept Skye so busy that she wasn't able to frequent Humbled as much as she would've liked. She missed their school days when they would see each other almost every day. Life had been much simpler back then.

She was waiting for Molly to notice Lula when her best friend suddenly let out a gasp. "So the rumors are true," Molly said, her brows knitting together.

"You've heard rumors?" Skye asked. Why was she surprised? Gossip flew on the wind in Serenity Peak.

Molly rolled her eyes. "Don't act like you don't know how this place works. I love our hometown, but there are no secrets here." Molly bent over and gazed at Lula in the stroller. The baby was wide-awake, her eyes taking everything in. "She's adorable. I can't believe you didn't tell me about finding her."

Skye squeezed her friend's arm. "I'm sorry, but yesterday was a whirlwind. We had the state trooper's office out at the property and everything unfolded very quickly. It was all such a shock."

"Okay, I understand. But I want all the details. Grab a seat and I'll swing by with your order. Your regular, right? A chai latte with a cinnamon bun and a croissant to take home."

Skye grinned. "You know me well." She walked over to a corner table and settled in while making sure Lula was content. She had brought a bottle, diapers and a few rattles along in case the baby got fussy or needed to be changed. So far, Lula was being very agreeable.

A few minutes later, Molly joined her and Lula at the table.

"Greta's manning the fort for a few minutes. Tell me all about the baby," Molly said, sounding breathless.

Over coffee and pastries, Skye told her friend about finding Lula on the porch of Sugar's Place.

"And you have no idea who might have left her there?" Molly asked.

Skye shook her head. "I've been racking my brain, but I honestly have no clue." She took a sip of her savory latte. She didn't say it out loud, but last night her mind had been racing with all the possibilities. Someone struggling to raise other kids? A young girl?

Molly nibbled on her croissant. "Some folks are speculating that it could be an employee of Sugar Works."

Molly's comment caught her off guard. She hadn't considered this possibility at all, but it made sense. In a small town like Serenity Peak, she knew all the workers on a first-name basis, but as she'd come to learn, that didn't mean she knew what was going on in their lives.

"To be honest, Molly, anything's possible. There

wasn't a person in sight when I found her, but I could have missed seeing someone if they were hiding behind the trees," Skye explained. "Everything happened so fast."

"It's incredible, really, considering the low temps," Molly said in a shocked tone.

"I have to think the person was watching for me to arrive and then placed Lula on the porch. Nothing else makes sense," Skye explained. "She's in great shape."

"Well, we need to continue this conversation later. I've got to get back to work," Molly said, getting up from her seat and looking around the bustling café.

"Come for dinner next week," Skye called out to Molly, who gave her a thumbs-up sign in response. Skye turned toward Lula, who gifted her with a gummy smile and a gurgling noise. "I guess it's just the two of us now."

"Skye." The deep voice caused her to swing her gaze up. Ryan. He was standing by her table with a to-go coffee cup in his hand, along with a bag that had the Humbled insignia printed on it. Dressed in his crisp state trooper's uniform, he looked way more attractive than she wanted to admit.

"How's everything going?" he asked, smiling at Lula. He reached out and grasped the baby's fingers. "She looks great." The way he was gazing down at Lula reminded her of the sweet Ryan she'd grown up with—the one she'd trusted and admired before everything shifted between them. When Ryan had started hanging around with a bad crowd in his early twenties and began getting into trouble, their friendship had fractured. She had tried to give him sound advice but he had rejected all of her help. As a result, they had drifted apart.

"She's doing well," Skye said. "Any word on a foster family?"

"We're working on it," Ryan said. "Mind if I sit down? I need to ask you something."

Skye couldn't very well say no, even though it felt a bit awkward to drink coffee with Ryan as if they were still buddies. Despite her mixed feelings about him, she needed to be civil since he was in charge of Lula's case. *Be the better person.* Her father's voice rang in her ears.

She would simply focus on Lula for the duration of their conversation and not dwell on the past. She would do anything for this sweet child who was growing on her by leaps and bounds.

Ryan sank down across from her and wrapped his hands around his coffee cup. Their eyes locked and she felt a funny little jolt in her midsection. There was no denying his masculine appeal.

"When I was out at Sugar's Place yesterday, I

searched the perimeter to see if anything turned up." He reached into his jacket pocket and pulled out a clear plastic baggie. "I found this outside in the snow. Is it yours?"

Ryan placed the bag, which held a shiny brass button, on the table and slid it toward her. Skye reached out and picked it up so she could examine it. After a few seconds she shook her head. "No, it's not mine."

"Well, I think it might belong to whoever left Lula at your place. The night before last it snowed. That button was on top of the snow, which means it was left sometime early yesterday."

Skye fingered the button. She had seen dozens exactly like this one over the years. She looked up and met Ryan's gaze. "I agree." She handed the button back to him. "And I'm pretty sure that I know where this came from."

Ryan leaned across the table and took back the button. "You do?" he asked, his voice full of surprise. The object had looked familiar to him, but he hadn't been able to place it.

Skye nodded. Her eyes were wide and solemn. "Unless I'm mistaken, this button is part of the cloak for Serenity Church's choir. I used to be a member. My sister was also a member before Chase was born."

He let out a surprised sound. Of course. Dozens of women in Serenity Peak belonged to the women's choir. His own mother had sung with them before her abrupt departure from town. Ryan shrugged off the memories of his mom, unwilling to give in to the overwhelming emotions they brought up.

"You're right," he said, shaking his head in disbelief. "I can't believe I didn't place it."

From what he remembered, Skye had stopped singing with the choir after Tyler called off the wedding. It had been sad to see her withdraw from her usual social activities. Thanks to Tyler's actions, Skye's bright light had been snuffed out. He had to wonder if the old Skye would ever come back, the one who'd radiated pure joy and sunshine.Skye furrowed her brow. "Do you think that Lula's mother might be a choir member?"

He shrugged. The last thing he wanted was for rumors to spread around town about the possible identity of the baby's mother. It wouldn't be fair to have the town speculating and pointing fingers. Knee-jerk reactions tended to hurt a lot of people.

"It's impossible to know as of yet," he explained. "I only mentioned it just in case the button belonged to you. I'm going to ask that you keep this conversation private. We don't need folks to start a whisper campaign. The button may not mean anything at all."

Skye nodded. "I understand, Ryan." Her mouth twisted. "I know what it's like to be the subject of rumors. I'd never want to do that to anyone else."

Ryan winced. From the tone of Skye's voice, the aftermath of her canceled wedding had been brutal. For what felt like the millionth time, anger at Tyler rose up inside of him. Although they'd always been the best of friends, Ryan had thoroughly disapproved of how Tyler had treated Skye. He also didn't like Tyler's out-of-control partying and chaotic lifestyle. For years their friendship had been rocky. Ryan had turned his life around and gotten into law enforcement. He was done with being reckless and irresponsible. Since Skye had stayed away from town for the last few years, she probably had no idea that his friendship with her ex-fiancé had splintered.

"I'm sorry that happened to you," he said. His heart went out to her. Up until that point she'd lived a pretty tranquil existence in Serenity Peak. Adored by the entire town. Coddled by her family.

Skye opened her mouth, then quickly closed it. She abruptly stood up, reached for her purse and looped it over her shoulder. She paused to pick up the to-go box. Her movements were jerky. "I need to get going," she said, stepping behind the stroller and hastily pushing it away from the table.

Ryan sputtered. He couldn't believe she'd just up and left him. What was her problem with him? Frankly, there was no time like the present to find out. He stood up and followed her, catching up with her just as she made her way outside the doors.

"Skye!" he called out. "Hold on."

She turned around with a look of surprise etched on her face. "What is it?"

He took a few steps toward her until there were only a few inches between them. Ryan shifted from one foot to the other, then shoved a hand through his dark hair,

"We used to be friends, didn't we?" he asked. "This is a fairly small town and we grew up together. What exactly did I do to make you hate me so much?"

"I—I don't know what you're talking about." Skye's denial came out in a flat monotone. She looked away from him.

"Oh, but I think you do," Ryan said. "Just tell me. Give it to me straight."

Skye let out a frustrated sound. "This isn't the time or the place."

He let out a ragged sigh. All he wanted to do was clear the air between them. Serenity Peak was too small a town for Skye to have an issue with him. It would be ridiculous to continue to avoid one another, especially now that there was the matter of Lula. "No time like the present. We need to talk this out since we're working together to make sure Lula has a great home."

She threw her hands in the air. "Okay! If you want to know so badly, it's because you disparaged me to Tyler." Skye let out a huff of air. "Don't get me wrong. I fell out of love with him a long time ago, but it still makes me angry that you badmouthed me right before the wedding."

Skye's words blew Ryan away. He couldn't have been more surprised if she'd knocked him over. She thought he'd gotten in the way of her wedding to Tyler?

"What are you talking about? You lost me." Ryan was genuinely confused. All he'd ever done was be a sounding board for Tyler as any friend would. And he'd never badmouthed Skye. *Why would I?* As far as he'd been concerned, Tyler had been a bit out of his league with Skye Drummond. His friend would have been fortunate to marry such an incredible woman. Yet he'd let her go.

Her lips trembled. "Tyler told me what you said. That I wasn't mature enough to be his wife. And that I wasn't ready for marriage. He cited those words when he called off the ceremony." Skye held her head up high, but her chin wobbled.

Ryan couldn't believe what he was hearing. "He said what? That's ridiculous. I never said that about you, nor did I ever think it." He had no idea if Skye believed him, but he was telling the truth. Downing people wasn't his style. And he had always held Skye in high esteem. It bothered him that Tyler had blamed him to take the heat off himself.

"Whether you want to believe it or not, Tyler always had a bad habit of blaming others for his own actions. He's been doing it ever since we were kids." He clenched his fists at his side as old memories resurfaced. "He would break out a window with a baseball and blame the rest of us. That's who he's always been, Skye. He's masterful at scapegoating."

Their gazes locked and held. Skye seemed to be pondering what he'd said to her. Maybe, just maybe, she sensed he was being truthful. Then again, she had always been blind when it came to Tyler. He really shouldn't judge her since he'd put up with Tyler for far too long himself.

"I've always been a truthful person, Skye, despite my faults. You used to know that. You used to know me." He shook his head. "That's not my style at all."

Suddenly Ryan's cell began to buzz insistently. He looked down at his phone, instantly recognizing the number on the screen. "I need to take this," he told her. "It'll just be a moment."

Ryan turned away from Skye so he could speak privately. "Hey, Gideon. What's going on?"

Less than a minute later he'd finished with the call. He was a little surprised that Skye was still standing on the sidewalk, waiting for him. She was pushing the stroller back and forth as if Lula needed soothing.

"That was Gideon," he explained. "He spoke with our contact in Homer. They've found a foster family that can take Lula."

Skye let out a startled sound and her eyes went wide. She appeared to be unsettled by the news, even though this development wasn't unusual in these situations.

"According to Gideon, everything is going to move very fast now," Ryan said. The baby would be transported out of town, and some instinct told him that Skye needed to prepare herself for Lula's departure.

Skye looked down at Lula. "You hear that, sweetie? It's such good news." The upbeat words coming out of her mouth didn't match her sad expression.

"Well, I've got to head back to the office and help Gideon with the arrangements. I'll be in touch shortly," Ryan said with a nod before walking toward his vehicle. There was no point in resurrecting their discussion about her negative feelings toward him. At this point she was going to believe what she wanted. And she believed he'd criticized her. Put a wedge between her and Tyler.

Just as he was about to get in his vehicle, Ryan heard Skye's voice calling after him. He turned to see her rushing toward him with a slightly panicked expression on her face. Emotion shimmered in her eyes.

"Please don't send Lula away, Ryan," Skye beseeched him. "I—I want to be her foster mom."

Chapter Four

Skye didn't think she'd ever seen Ryan speechless before. Ever since they were little kids, he'd been a chatterbox. She recalled him getting into trouble with their fourth grade teacher, Miss Smythe, for that very reason.

"Did you hear what I said?" she asked.

Almost instantly, his eyes widened. "C-come again?" Ryan stumbled over his words.

"I want to be Lula's foster mom." She met his gaze head-on, without blinking, and kept her voice steady. More than anything, Ryan needed to know she was serious. Despite the way it might appear, this wasn't a passing fancy or an overreaction to the situation. Skye was being called to step in the breach for this precious baby. The dream of being a foster parent had been nestled in her heart since childhood.

He frowned at her. A look of incredulity settled on his face.

"You? You want to foster the baby?" Ryan asked, shock ringing out in his voice.

Her heart sank. She might has well have said that aliens had just touched down in Moose Falls. Why was it so hard for him to believe her?

"It's not that surprising," she said, folding her arms across her chest. "I found her on the steps of Sugar's Place. My gut is telling me that someone left her there so I would discover her."

"We don't know that for sure," he cautioned, holding up his hands. "But I agree with you. More than likely the person who left Lula on your property knew she would be in good hands with you."

Skye's chest tightened upon hearing Ryan's reassuring comment. Suddenly it all came back to her—how he had been the sweetest boy in school and everyone's buddy. Matter of fact, she had confided in him that she wanted to foster a child one day. How could she have forgotten that? She chided herself.

"Do you remember my telling you about my dream of fostering a child? Back in high school?" Skye asked, praying he would say yes.

A grin tugged at his lips. "It's been a long time, but I do recall that particular wish of yours. You wanted to walk in Sugar's footsteps."

The mention of her mother caused a groundswell of emotion to rise up inside of her. The fact that he remembered something so personal and precious meant the world to her. And now, standing here face-to-face with Ryan, Skye had to acknowledge the fact that her anger toward him had been misplaced. She had been in the wrong, all because of Tyler's manipulations.

Ryan's a good man. Her father's words came back to remind her of something she'd always known. Shame rose up inside of her. She had been treating Ryan unfairly. All of the anger she had been holding on to began to dissipate. If she was going to foster Lula, she needed Ryan in her corner.

"Thank you for hearing me out," she murmured, overcome by gratitude. It meant a lot to her that Ryan also believed it wasn't a coincidence that her family's property had been chosen as a safe haven and that he recalled her dream of being a foster mother.

Ryan shifted from one foot to the other. "It's not as easy as a simple request, though. You have to be certified as a foster parent. That can't happen overnight."

"But my family has that status and my dad has kept up with his certification. I would qualify since we've fostered on numerous occasions," Skye said. She prayed that her family's fostering history worked in her favor. Surely it had to count for something?

Ryan narrowed his gaze. "Have you even run this by Abel?"

Skye bit her lip. The idea to foster Lula for an extended period had come to her like a bolt from the blue. She hadn't had the time to tell her father about it. And frankly, she wasn't sure what his reaction would be. He'd needed some convincing to agree to the short-term placement. He was a loving, giving man, but he also had a thriving business to nurture. Most likely, he wouldn't have time to devote to Lula's care. "I haven't," she admitted.

"I think you're going to need Abel on board since I'm assuming the certification is under his name." Ryan seemed to be thinking things through, which she took as a good sign.

"So, is it possible? Will I qualify?" Skye's heart began to thump fast and furious. Was this really possible?

Ryan nodded. "I think if Abel agrees to co-foster with you and is legally responsible for Lula's care, it could work."

She let out a little squeal, then quickly looked over at Lula to make sure she hadn't woken her. Thankfully, she was still resting peacefully. So far the baby was proving to be a real sweetheart with a wonderful disposition. The thought of weathering more sleepless nights didn't scare her one bit.

Skye touched her cheeks, aware that her emotions were spreading to her face. All of a sudden she was grinning at Ryan. "I'm going to head home right now and talk to my father. I'm praying this all works out."

"Me too," Ryan said with a nod. "I need to run this by Gideon, too, to see if it will pass muster. As soon as I get an answer I'll let you know."

On the way home Skye began to practice the speech she was planning to deliver to her father. Even though her decision to foster Lula had been swift, Skye had already worked out some of the details in her head.

The moment she spotted the gold-and-cream sign welcoming her to Sugar Works, she let out the breath she'd been holding. Maybe if she spoke to Violet first she could get her sister to support her plan. There was no way in the world their father could resist a plea from both of his daughters. A sense of pride filled her as she drove through the property on her way to the family homestead. Birch trees—the source of the syrup made by Sugar Works—were everywhere.

As she drove past the general store named after her mother, Skye felt a rush of longing. She missed her mother each and every day. Grief wasn't something a person could just neatly tuck away in a drawer. It swept over her at unexpected times, causing a deep ache in her soul. Sugar Drummond had been a force of nature—determined, caring and dedicated. A one-of-a-kind woman who had loved others just as fiercely as she had been loved.

The Drummonds' two-story log cabin–style home quickly came into view as she rounded the bend. *Home.* It was still her safe haven from the storms of life. Being here always made her feel loved and cherished. Maybe she could instill that same feeling in Lula if given the opportunity. Two figures—a child and an adult—were standing in the yard, throwing snowballs at each other. Seeing Violet and her nephew, Chase, sharing a fun-loving moment caused tears to pool in her eyes. As a single mother, Violet had strived to create a wonderful world for her son in the absence of the boy's father. In Skye's opinion, she was doing an incredible job raising Chase.

Mother and son looked nothing alike. Violet was tall, with strawberry blond hair and delicate features. Chase had dark, curly hair and olive skin. Her sister didn't talk much about Chase's father or what had transpired between them nearly a decade ago. They had enjoyed a whirlwind romance that culminated in an impulsive engagement a few weeks later. Before anyone had even known about their plans, John had beat a fast path out of Serenity Peak. All Skye knew was that he'd written her sister a brief goodbye letter before leaving without a trace.

Skye hated what he had done to Violet. Her sister had fallen in love with him, and he'd abandoned her after promising to stick beside her for a lifetime. In the aftermath, Violet's world had imploded. A few months after John's disappearing act, Violet had discovered she was pregnant with his baby. To her credit, she had dried her tears and focused on the child. She had held her head high despite cruel town gossip and the rigors of single parenthood.

After parking her vehicle, Skye spent a few moments taking Lula's baby carrier out of the back seat. She was immediately swarmed by Chase, with her sister following on his heels.

"Easy there, kiddo," Violet said, pulling on her son's coat to rein him in. "You need to be gentle around babies."

"Oops. I forgot," Chase said sheepishly, dragging his booted foot in the snow. Her nephew was on the quiet side for a nine-year-old boy and Skye often wondered what thoughts were whirling around in his head.

"That's okay," Skye reassured him. "No harm done." She playfully tweaked him on the chin.

"She's such a sweet girl," Violet said as she gazed down at Lula. She reached out and grazed her palm against the baby's cheek. "And quite the beauty."

"Isn't she?" Skye asked. "I should get her inside where it's warm." The last thing she wanted was for Lula to be exposed to the elements for an extended period of time. Her desire to protect this precious baby was unlike anything she'd ever experienced.

"You promised me chocolate chip cookies for an afternoon snack," Chase yelled as he ran toward the house. Violet chuckled at the sight of Chase racing through the front door.

"I'm starting to think he has a tapeworm. He's always hungry," Violet said, shaking her head. "Not to mention he's always outgrowing his clothes."

Skye knew her nephew took after his father with his dark hair and coloring. She wondered how long it would be before Chase began asking serious questions about the identity of his father. At his age such inquiries were to be expected.

"I need to run something important by you," Skye told Violet as they made their way toward the house. "It can't wait."

Her sister turned to her. "Sounds serious. Let me put the kettle on so you can tell me all about it over tea."

Once they were inside, the sisters headed to the kitchen. Chase, who was standing by the counter, held up two chocolate chip cookies and said, "This is going to help me with my times tables. Brain fuel," before scooting off toward the downstairs playroom.

The sisters chuckled in unison. Chase brought a lot of laughter into their lives, as well as nine-year-old mischief. His antics had lifted Skye up at her lowest points.

Violet made them tea while Skye heated up a bottle for Lula and changed her diaper. It was amazing how many diapers she'd gone through so far today. Skye settled the baby into a portable playpen that had once belonged to Chase and watched from a few feet away as Lula played with a mobile.

With cups of herbal tea in front of them, Skye quickly got Violet up to speed on her plan to foster Lula, and how she needed assistance convincing their father to support the proposal. Upon hearing the news, Violet's eyes rounded and she placed her teacup firmly down on the saucer.

"You look surprised," Skye said, noting the startled expression on her sister's face.

"Honestly, I am. Are you sure you're up to this?" Violet asked, a crease marring her forehead.

Skye told herself not to get upset over Violet's comment. She knew her sister always sought to protect her, first and foremost. Violet was always in big-sister mode, especially after Skye's heartbreak with Tyler and her self-imposed exile from town.

"You don't think I can serve that role?" Skye asked, her voice trembling. She steeled herself for the answer, reminding herself not to take it personally.

Violet reached out and patted her hand. "No, I didn't mean you're not capable, but you've been through the emotional ringer the last few years. You're just now getting your life back. You've been so excited about your new role as manager at Sugar's Place. How's that going to work?"

"I'll figure something out regarding the shop. I'm not taking any backward steps by fostering Lula." She grinned at Violet. "Matter of fact, it's a huge step forward. I haven't felt this hopeful or joyful in years. I'm stepping out on a limb of faith and believing that this is the right decision. It feels nice to trust my gut."

Tears pooled in her sister's eyes. Between the two of them, Skye was never certain which one of them was more emotional. "Oh, Skye. That's wonderful to hear. I didn't mean to doubt you. I just wanted to make sure you're in a place to take this on." She jumped up from her seat and walked around the butcher-block table to envelop Skye in a tight hug.

"Violet, I always know you're coming from a place of love," Skye said. "And you've been a second mother to me since Mama died. So much of what I've learned stems from your nurturing ways."

"You're going to be a great foster mother." Violet's face lit up with a huge grin. "And I can be her foster auntie and spoil her."

Skye crossed her hands in front of her. "I'm praying it all works out. You need to help me convince Dad to get on board. He's the one with the certification."

"Let's make him his favorite meal and go from there," Violet suggested with a wink.

Skye chuckled. "Are we trying to sway him through his love of food?"

"Don't laugh," Violet said, wrinkling her nose. "He'll do just about anything if you make him spaghetti Bolognese."

Although she wasn't against cooking for their father, Skye really wanted him to embrace the idea of her fostering Lula without any enticements. Her father's good opinion meant the world to her. If he approved of her plan, she would be filled with confidence. As much as she wanted to foster Lula, there was a small voice in her head that was making her doubt herself.

Before dinner, Skye brought Lula upstairs, laid her on the bed and changed her into one of her new outfits. Lula kicked her legs and arms, putting up a delightful fight when Skye tried to put the jumpsuit on. By the time she'd finished, both she and Lula were giggling. The sound of Lula's tinkling laughter went straight to Skye's heart and nestled there. "You look beautiful," Skye said as she admired the baby in her lavender outfit decorated with butterflies. "My daddy won't be able to refuse us now." She scooped Lula up and headed back downstairs to prep dinner.

By the time Abel walked through the door, the house smelled of garlic, baked bread and pasta. Skye gave him a few minutes to unwind before ushering him into the dining room for dinner.

"You've really outdone yourselves," Abel raved. "Everything smells heavenly."

As they all settled in around the table—with Lula placed in Chase's old high chair since she was able to sit up—they held hands and prayed over the food. Skye had pureed some sweet potatoes and peas for Lula, who didn't hesitate to grab a handful and push the veggies in her mouth.

Just as they were about to dig into the meal, the doorbell rang.

"I'll get it," Chase said, jumping up from his seat. He raced off to open the door, full of his usual energy. Skye heard the low rumble of a man's voice. Seconds later Chase reappeared with Ryan at his side. He was still wearing his state trooper's uniform, which meant this was official business.

A sinking feeling coursed through Skye. Her heart seized up at the sight of him.

Had Ryan stopped by to bring bad news from Gideon about Lula?

Ryan's stomach growled in appreciation as he stood in the Drummonds' dining room inhaling the scent of pasta and freshly baked bread. He chided himself for showing up without warning just as the Drummonds were gathering for dinner. He'd just spoken to Gideon and urgently needed an update from Skye, who hadn't answered his calls. Knowing how important this was to Skye had lit a fire under him. Time was of the essence. To make the situation more complicated, the foster parent situation in Homer had fallen apart. Lula truly didn't have a place to go at the moment, which made Abel's decision all the more crucial.

"Ryan. What brings you out here?" Abel asked. "It's great seeing you but it has me wondering if this is a social call or official business."

"I wanted to talk to Skye about Lula," he said, swinging his gaze over to Skye.

Skye looked back at him with wide eyes, clearly imploring him to not spill the beans in front of Abel. Ryan immediately picked up on her cues. Judging by the nervous expression on her face, she hadn't yet broached the topic with her father. Uh-oh. By coming over here, he had stepped right into it. Thankfully, he hadn't said anything revealing.

"I tried to reach you by phone, but you didn't pick up the calls," he said. "I apologize for showing up unannounced."

"Oh, I'm sorry about that. We were cooking and I must have had my ringer off," Skye explained.

"Take a seat, Ryan. There's enough Bolognese to feed a small village," Abel said, beckoning him toward the table.

"I don't want to impose," he said, feeling sheepish. Why did being in Skye's presence always rattle him so much? Even though he was good at being a trooper, she made him feel like a teenage boy all over again.

Abel let out a heavy sigh. "Please sit down with us. Considering the fact that my daughters made my favorite meal and it's not my birthday, I have the feeling something's up." He gestured for Ryan to sit down in the seat next to Skye. Once he did so, Violet quickly brought him a plate and utensils.

As Ryan began filling his plate, Abel looked around the table. "Okay, who's going to tell me what's going on? I was born at night, but I wasn't born last night."

Chase let out a loud cackle of laughter. "That's a good one, Gramps." He slapped his hand on the table. "You weren't born last night."

If the situation hadn't been so serious, Ryan might have laughed out loud at Abel's comment right along with Chase. Tension crackled in the very air around them. It was palpable.

A few moments of silence occurred without anyone speaking. Skye cleared her throat. "Daddy, it's about Lula." She reached over and smoothed Lula's curls. "I know this might sound surprising, but I want to foster her." She bit her lip. "Since I don't have the certification yet, you're going to have to be involved as a co-foster parent if this is going to be approved."

Abel ran his hand across his beard. He seemed to be deep in thought.

"Are you going to get certified?" Abel asked, his gaze narrowing as he looked at his daughter.

"Yes, I'm planning to start doing the requisite work to obtain certification, but as Ryan can attest to, time is of the essence." Her voice wavered and tears gathered in her eyes. "The plan is to send Lula to a foster family in Homer right away. But there's a chance we can foster her instead."

Abel steepled his hands in front of him. He looked over at Ryan with a frown on his face. "What's your take on all this?"

"I discussed Skye's plan with Gideon, and as I thought, the decision lies with you, Abel. If you're on board as Lula's foster parent and she's legally in your care, Gideon will sign off on it." He grinned at Abel. "You have an outstanding history of fostering children. Skye will qualify under the umbrella of your having been a foster family, but to approve this we need to cross all the *t*'s with certification. That means you have to sign on the dotted line since Skye isn't yet certified." Ryan paused. "And there's been a slight hitch... The foster family in Homer pulled out due to a family emergency."

"Oh no!" Skye exclaimed. She turned toward her father. "Lula needs us more than ever now."

"You're really determined to do this, aren't you?" Abel asked her. "And you don't have any reservations?"

Skye nodded. "I am. I've always enjoyed being part of a foster family, and deep inside of me I've always known it was something I wanted to pursue when I got older." A sweet smile lit up her face. "That's because of you. And I promise I'll be doing the bulk of the work. I know most of your days are filled up with Sugar Works and the birch trees. I'll be the main caregiver." Skye was working overtime to present a compelling case to Abel. Ryan couldn't tell by her father's shuttered expression if it was working or not.

"I'll help out as much as I can," Violet added. "And we can give Kira additional hours at Sugar's Place so Skye won't have to work as many shifts. That way she can really focus on Lula's needs and get the baby on a schedule."

"I can help, too," Chase chimed in. "It'll be good for me to have a foster sister since I'm an only child. I can make a list of all the things she needs to learn."

Violet leaned over and placed a kiss on his cheek. "You're the best, kiddo."

Another moment of silence hung in the air.

"Daddy, you're not saying much," Skye said. Her hands were crossed prayerfully in front of her. "What are you thinking?"

"Skye, being entrusted with a child's welfare is one of the biggest assignments a person could ever be given," Abel said. "It requires patience and dedication. And most of all, a desire to love and protect a child who's not your own. A foster parent has to have a heart that grows and expands each and every day. It just might be the most challenging undertaking of your life." He drew a deep breath. "Sweetheart, you're more than worthy of the task. Honestly, I can't think of anyone other than Violet who is more prepared to love and nurture a precious baby. You have my approval. And my support."

Skye let out a squeal and raised her hands

in the air. "I won't disappoint you. Most of all, I'm not going to let Lula down." At the sound of her name, Lula let out a gurgling sound and smiled. Everyone laughed as they looked over at the adorable baby who seemed as if she didn't have a care in the world. Ryan wondered if she was missing her parents or questioning why her world had changed so dramatically. It was rather astounding how children were so resilient.

"Well, it's settled, then," Abel announced. "Let's dig in before the food is stone-cold." He began to eat his dinner with gusto.

"You don't have to tell me twice," Ryan said as he swirled spaghetti on his fork before placing it in his mouth. He had worked straight through lunch and only managed to eat a few bites of his sandwich from Humbled. He'd been too preoccupied with the foster baby situation to eat much. As the pasta hit his taste buds Ryan wanted to let out a sound of appreciation for the meal. The dish was savory and delicious.

A festive mood hung in the air as they enjoyed the meal together. Skye looked over the moon with happiness. And somehow, that made him feel joyful. Being in the midst of a family supper made him nostalgic for the old days when his own folks had been happily married. His aunt Mary and cousin Zane had been alive then. His family hadn't been perfect, but they'd all been together. Grief and loss had taken a toll on all of them.

At the end of dinner, Ryan decided to excuse himself before dessert was served. He didn't want to overstay his welcome or intrude on Skye's celebratory mood any longer.

He stood up from the table. "I hate to eat and run, but I'm going to head home. Autumn, Judah and the baby are in Skagway, so I'm dog-sitting Delilah for them." His uncle Judah, a local fisherman, had recently married his former sweetheart, Autumn Hines. After a long absence, Autumn had returned to Serenity Peak, pregnant and divorced. They'd reunited and gotten married shortly after baby River's birth.

"Oh, I love Delilah. Can I come see her sometime?" Chase asked. He seemed so excited about the Irish setter, Ryan couldn't bear to say no to him.

"Well, I could bring her by in the next few days if that's okay with your mom," Ryan said, shooting a glance at Violet.

"We would love that," Violet said. "Chase has been asking me for a dog for months now, so this will give him some face time with an actual dog while we figure out the specifics." Chase was grinning from ear to ear and rubbing his hands together with excitement.

"Let me walk you to the door," Skye suggested, jumping to her feet and scooping up Lula in her arms. "I think someone needs to go to sleep soon. She's fading fast."

Once they reached the front door, Ryan cleared his throat and turned to face Skye. He shifted from one foot to the other. "There's something else I need to tell you. Gideon wants me to be in the loop since he bent over backward to approve the situation."

Skye's brows drew together. "What does that mean?"

"It means I'm going to be a permanent fixture around here until you obtain the certification. Don't take it personally, but I'll be checking in on you and Lula several times a week. Consider me her honorary foster uncle."

Chapter Five

It means I'm going to be a permanent fixture around here.

Skye couldn't count the number of times she had replayed Ryan's words in her head. It still gave her goose bumps. She had tried to hide her dismay from Ryan as much as possible last night when he'd delivered the news to her. Honestly, she wasn't sure why Gideon wanted Ryan to keep an eye on her fostering skills in the first place. It was a tad insulting. Ryan had gone on to explain that with her father and Violet working long hours, it was the only way Gideon could justify granting her foster mom status without her certification.

She let out a sigh of frustration. Ryan had come through for her in ways she had never envisioned. He'd gone to bat for her with Gideon and paved the way for her to become Lula's foster mother. Her gratitude overrode her irritation at the current situation. How could she be annoyed at Ryan after all he'd done to help her? Furthermore, he was only following directions from his boss. Clearly, Gideon thought she needed someone peering over her shoulder, even though she had plenty of experience with babies. Maybe he was just making sure that no trouble arose from the decision to allow her to foster Lula.

She was going to make the best of the situation and work toward earning her certification quickly. That way no one could argue that she didn't have the proper skills to be a foster mom. With every passing day that she spent with Lula, Skye felt her heart expanding by leaps and bounds. Babies were so precious and vulnerable. For the first time in her life, she felt needed. She had a role to play—an important one that had nothing to do with her looks or being well-liked in Serenity Peak.

She was on her way to town to drop off a few baskets of goods from Sugar's Place at Northern Lights restaurant for their fundraiser. Skye had just completed a three-hour shift at the general store, and she'd figured out ways to keep Lula entertained for short bursts of time while she waited on customers. Using a playpen and a baby swing had allowed her to make sales and restock the shelves.

It was a gorgeous day to make the drive into town. The sky was clear and a stunning shade of cerulean blue. Skye knew she was fortunate to live in Alaska. Wide-open spaces. Breathtaking vistas. Snowcapped mountains. Plenty of fresh air. Serenity Peak had always been a sanctuary for folks seeking peace and tranquility. The town had an abundance of businesses specializing in wellness and creative endeavors. Artists. Writers. Jewelry makers and chefs. As well as being the creator of Sugar Works, her father was a master craftsman. Just recently he'd made a cradle for Violet's best friend, Autumn. Her husband, Judah, happened to be Ryan's uncle.

Driving up to the restaurant was quite an experience. Northern Lights sat atop a cliff that provided stunning views of Kachemak Bay and the Serenity Mountains. It was one of the most spectacular views in Serenity Peak, one she'd missed a lot.

As soon as she entered the establishment, Sean Hines, Autumn's brother and the restaurant's owner, greeted her with a welcoming bear hug. A former professional football player, he had the physique of a linebacker and warm brown skin. With his charming disposition, Sean was beloved in town.

"It's been a long time, Skye. I've missed seeing that smile of yours."

"It has been," Skye acknowledged. Ever since Tyler called off the wedding, Skye had kept a low profile, mainly due to embarrassment and shame. Only recently had she come out of her self-imposed isolation. Why had she ever considered Tyler's change of heart to be her disgrace? She had placed the blame squarely on her own shoulders and allowed the opinions of others to influence her thinking.

It didn't take Sean long to comment on Lula. "Who's your sidekick?" he asked, grinning.

Skye quickly got him up to speed on the situation. A range of emotions passed over his face as she spoke. By the end, he was nodding with approval.

"So you're a foster mom now, huh?" he asked, beaming at her. "Following in the family tradition, I see."

She smiled back at him. "It's a bit surreal, but I am." Foster mom. She loved the sound of those words. She was already over the moon about Lula. "I couldn't juggle Lula and the baskets, so I figured someone could give me a hand."

"I could have picked up the baskets myself rather than have you trek into town with the baby to drop them off," he said, shaking his head. "I had no idea."

"It's okay," she said. "Lula is pretty good-natured and it gave me a chance to experience the breathtaking view from outside. That never gets old."

"God's masterpiece," Sean said. "Let me go outside and bring the baskets in. I know they'll be a big hit."

"Thanks, Sean. My car is right by the back door."

After Sean walked down the hall, Skye looked around the place, admiring the recent renovations and the cream-and-baby blue decor that provided a warm, welcoming vibe. "This place looks really nice, Lula. What do you think?" At the sound of her name, Lula began babbling, her face upturned to Skye. Moments like this one tugged at Skye's heartstrings. It would only be a matter of time until Lula was talking up a storm and walking. Children grew up really quickly and she intended to savor these moments as long as possible. There was no telling when a permanent situation for Lula would arise. A family might seek to adopt her, or her birth parents could resurface. Although it would be nice to foster Lula long-term, she wasn't in control of the situation. All she could do was pray for Lula's well-being.

"Long time no see," a high-pitched voice called out to Skye.

Cici Hines, Sean and Autumn's sister, made a beeline in Skye's direction. Cici worked as a waitress at Northern Lights. Bubbly and talkative, she had a reputation for being a chatterbox.

Skye knew she meant well, but she had no intention of dishing out any major details about Lula.

"So this is the little lady who's been causing all the talk in town," Cici said as she peered down at Lula. "She's adorable."

A sigh slipped past her lips. She wasn't at all surprised that Lula was the topic of conversation. "I can't argue with that. Lula is a beautiful baby," Skye said. "So, what are people saying?" she asked, curiosity overtaking her.

Cici shrugged. "A lot of people are speculating about where she came from and who dropped her off at the general store."

"It could remain a mystery unless someone steps forward," Skye responded. She couldn't help but think about the button that Ryan had found a few feet away from Sugar's Place. It really could be the only clue as to the identity of the person who'd dropped off Lula. Skye wasn't about to convey that information to Cici. Ryan has asked her to keep it confidential, which was fine by her.

"Gossip aside, I'm happy to see you out and about," Cici said. "This town needs your sweet energy."

Skye appreciated Cici's kindness. "Right back at you, Cici," she said with a grin.

Just then Skye spotted Ryan standing by the front entrance. She felt a quick burst of adrenaline flowing through her veins at the sight of him. Perhaps she should walk over and thank him for being so supportive and kind yesterday. She should have done so last night.

Before she could make a move, Skye noticed Ryan's companion. Standing right behind him was Tyler, who was laughing and acting as if he didn't have a care in the world. Her entire body froze up at the sight of him.

"Cici, it was nice seeing you. I have to run." She picked up Lula's carrier and beat a fast path to the back door. Once she was outside, Skye began gulping deep breaths of air. With trembling fingers, she secured Lula into her car seat, then quickly got behind the wheel.

Although she no longer loved her ex-fiancé, Skye didn't want to come face-to-face with him in one of the most popular establishments in town with townsfolk watching.

As she drove away from Northern Lights, all she could think about was how in one single moment, all the progress she'd made since being ditched at the altar had evaporated into thin air.

Ryan hadn't forgotten his promise to bring Delilah to visit with Chase at the Drummonds' place. It was late afternoon before he was able to leave the state trooper's office, head home to pick up Delilah, then drive over to the Drummonds.

As he entered the front gates and drove around the property toward the homestead, Ryan found himself admiring the Drummonds' awe-inspiring land. The sheer acreage was staggering. Birch trees were in abundance. Workers were packing materials into trucks. With spring mere weeks away, he knew they were gearing up for production and laying the foundation for that work.

He sincerely hoped Skye was all right. He had witnessed her bolting from Northern Lights earlier this afternoon when she'd seen Tyler. Ryan couldn't stop thinking about the uncomfortable expression stamped on her face right before she'd taken off. He'd only been there to pick up a takeout order, but he'd crossed paths with Tyler once he walked through the doors. Of course Skye probably assumed he had been hanging out with her ex, which couldn't be farther from the truth.

His first instinct had been to follow after her, but Ryan hadn't wanted to draw any attention to her hasty departure. As it was, the townsfolk were already flapping their jaws about Lula being dropped off at Sugar's Place. Theories were running rampant about the identity of Lula's mother and it had reached a fever pitch. He knew no good could come of all the talk, especially if folks ended up getting dragged into the situation due to unfounded speculation.

"Okay, Delilah, we're here," he announced to the Irish setter as the Drummond family home came into view. He followed the road leading toward a circular driveway in front of the house. After parking, he beeped his horn to announce his arrival, then jumped down from the truck with Delilah on his heels. A few moments later Chase came barreling out of the house, screaming at the top of his lungs.

"You're here!" the little boy shouted. "You didn't forget about me."

"Of course I didn't," Ryan said, tousling Chase's hair as he reached his side. "You're a pretty unforgettable kid."

Chase bent down and immediately began to pat Delilah. "Hey, girl. It's great to see you again. I don't know if you remember, but your dad brought you over here one day. We played for a long time." Delilah answered him by vigorously licking his face. Chase burst into giggles. The boy's love for canines was effusive.

"Chase," a voice called out. "You forgot your hat." Skye came striding toward them from the house, extending the red-and-gray knit cap to her nephew.

"Thanks, Auntie. I was so excited I forgot."

He looked up at Ryan. "Can I run Delilah over to my tree house?"

"Sure thing. Just make sure she doesn't wander off. She's not familiar with the property." He handed him Delilah's leash. "Just in case."

"And don't take Delilah up to the tree house," Skye said in a warning tone. "Keep her on the ground."

"I won't," Chase said as he called to Delilah, then took off running through the snow.

"He's a great kid," Ryan remarked as he watched Chase and the lovable Irish setter head toward the woods. He swung his gaze back toward Skye. She was bundled up in a pink parka and a pair of jeans. A cute white hat perched on her head. As always, she looked beautiful. Ryan had to remind himself not to stare.

"Lula's napping," she said, holding up a baby monitor. "I went into town earlier, so I think that tuckered her out."

A small sigh slipped past his lips. Did she think he was checking up on her? "You don't owe me an explanation. I don't expect her to be glued to your side at all times. And I only swung by to keep my promise to Chase."

A small smile crept across her face. "We're grateful to you for bringing Delilah by so Chase could spend time with her. He's been going through a bit of a hard time lately."

Although Ryan wanted to ask her what was going on with the boy, he knew if he did so it would be overstepping. He had reached a tenuous peace with Skye and he didn't want to take any backward steps. Lula had brought them together. Maybe they really could be friends again. Ryan would be grateful if they could rebuild their connection.

The thought of getting close to Skye again was a bit terrifying, if he was being honest with himself. Back in the day, right before she had paired up with Tyler, Ryan's feelings for her had deepened into something more than friendship. He had pushed those feelings aside and moved past them, but Ryan knew his heart might be vulnerable to Skye. He was ashamed of the way he had treated women in his past—casually and without care or affection. Since then he'd deliberately steered clear of any romantic entanglements as he did the hard work to turn his life around. Becoming a man of faith had inspired him to be a better man in all aspects of his life. Ryan still wondered if he could be a stable, loving partner.

"By the way, I saw you at Northern Lights," he blurted out. He couldn't get the thought of her disappearing act out of his mind. It was gnawing at him.

Her eyes went wide. "I—I didn't realize you saw me."

"I did. We just happened to be there at the same time, me and Tyler," he explained. "I haven't seen him in months."

Skye shook her head. "You don't have to justify anything to me. The two of you have been friends for a long time."

They had been close in the past. Over the last few years their tight bond had diminished. Tyler had been living a wild lifestyle that didn't gel with Ryan's current outlook as a state trooper. Ryan had been determined to lead a life of purpose while Tyler had chosen a different path for himself. Losing their friendship had been painful, but it hadn't happened overnight. Things had been unraveling for years, until Ryan could no longer justify continuing the friendship.

There was no point in explaining this to Skye. The less talk of her ex the better. At some point he would tell her that he and Tyler were no longer friends. Just not right now.

"I'm sorry if seeing Tyler was difficult. They say healing a broken heart can be a long process." Not that he knew from personal experience in a romantic relationship, but he'd seen his Uncle Judah struggle for years after losing his only child. Ryan had also been devastated by the loss of Aunt Mary and Zane.

Out of nowhere Skye let out a burst of laughter. Once she started she couldn't seem to stop. She raised her hand to cover her mouth. Finally, she said, "Sorry, but I couldn't help myself. I am *not* in love with Tyler anymore. I fell out of love with him a long time ago."

A feeling of relief flooded him. The thought of Skye pining away for Tyler didn't sit well with him. He didn't want to examine the reasons why.

He drew his brows together. "Then why did you bolt from the restaurant? I assumed it was because of Tyler being there."

"Yes, it was, but not for the reasons you think. In the beginning it hurt to see him, which is why I rarely ever left the property. Not to mention it was embarrassing to be a jilted bride." She looked away. "We've only crossed paths a few times, but every time we do, new rumors start popping up about us." She shook her head, her blond curls cascading around her shoulders. "It makes moving forward harder. So much speculation just made me uncomfortable."

"I understand. There are good folks here in Serenity Peak, but the residents also like to gossip. The truth is rarely a consideration." He knew it all too well. After his Aunt Mary and cousin Zane's fatal car crash, ugly, false rumors had circulated about his aunt being under the influence prior to the accident. It had led to misunderstandings and an estrangement between his father and Uncle Judah. Thankfully, they had reconciled.

"And now the talk has shifted to Lula. Everyone seems to have a running theory about her origins." She tilted her head. "I can't explain why but it makes me uncomfortable."

"I suppose talk is to be expected since it's not every day that a baby is left with no explanation whatsoever. I'm really struck by the fact that this happened to your family once before. I can't help but wonder if there's any connection."

"It is unusual. That's how my family got started with fostering. We all fell in love with the baby, especially my mother." A wistful expression crossed her face.

"The same way you're falling in love with Lula?" he asked.

"How can I not love her?" Skye asked. "She's adorable and easygoing. We bonded right away. And she needs me," she said in a soft voice. "She makes me feel as if I have a purpose. I'm not just taking up space."

Skye's admission shocked him. He would never have imagined that she felt this way. Even when they were kids, she'd possessed a single-minded determination and drive. Her kindness had endeared her to everyone. "Of course you have a purpose. We all do. I've struggled with those feelings myself, but in the last few years I've been able to get back on track."

"Yeah, you've come a long way, Ryan. Not too long ago you were the bad boy of Serenity Peak." She raised her eyebrow as if remembering his exploits.

That was putting it mildly, he thought. Ryan couldn't even take offense at the label. He had been completely out of control for years, running around with different women and drinking way past his limits. That was before he had given his life over to God and become a man of faith. As a result, his whole world had changed. Becoming a state trooper had given him a purpose and a vocation that he could be proud of.

"I made a lot of mistakes." He felt the back of his neck warm with embarrassment. "After losing Zane and Aunt Mary...and then my Mom taking off and divorcing my dad, I pretty much imploded. I was fortunate that folks still believed in me and allowed me to become a trooper."

"From what I've heard you've done a fine job. You've been a godsend with Lula. I won't ever forget how supportive you were. I owe you a huge debt of gratitude."

His chest swelled at the praise. Coming from someone he respected made it all the more heart-felt. For such a long time he'd struggled to move past his youthful mistakes. Now he had come out on the other side. "You're welcome. I wouldn't have done so if I didn't believe that you would be a great foster mother. Ever since we were kids you insisted on taking care of every broken-winged bird you came across." In his mind's eye he could see a pint-sized Skye nursing a baby owl back to health.

The sound of her tinkling laughter filled the space between them. The little crinkles around her eyes as she giggled drew his attention. He liked seeing Skye happy and glowing from within. For so long now her light had been dimmed. Now she was lit up like a lantern.

Her eyes twinkled. "I can't believe you remember that. I wanted to be a veterinarian or a nurse in the worst way. But to be honest with you, more than anything I wanted to be a mother. That idea was always firmly planted in my head."

Skye's words brought the entire situation into clear focus. She was getting more attached to Lula with every passing day. And although it wasn't a bad thing, he worried that she might get in over her head emotionally. If a suitable family stepped up to adopt Lula, Skye might be caught off guard.

"Just be mindful that fostering is really a temporary situation. As you know, it can end at any time," he cautioned. "You've got to be prepared for that eventuality."

"I get it," she said, sounding a bit curt. "But I'm going to savor these moments for as long as I can and make the most of being Lula's mother." Just then a loud cry rang out over the baby monitor. "I've got to run inside. Can you check on Chase for me?" she asked.

"Of course," he said. "Go see to Lula." Before the words were even out of his mouth, Skye was racing toward the house as if her feet were on fire.

Ryan frowned as his gaze trailed after her. He couldn't help but notice how Skye had called herself Lula's mother rather than her foster mother. Maybe it was simply a slip of the tongue. Perhaps he was nitpicking. He didn't want to borrow trouble, but he had a strong feeling that Skye had already become way more bonded to the baby than she realized.

He had a sinking feeling in his gut that this meant trouble.

Chapter Six

❧

"What do you think of this, Lula?" Skye asked as she held up the newest merchandise for her approval. The oatmeal-colored T-shirt had on it a Sugar Works logo surrounded by birch trees. So far, it was Skye's favorite piece of apparel since the artwork truly reflected her family's business and philosophy.

In response to the question, Lula's eyes widened, causing Skye to chuckle with amusement. "I'll take that as a yes," Skye said, placing a kiss on the baby's forehead. Lula gazed up at her and gurgled. Even though Lula didn't talk yet, Skye sensed she was trying her best to engage with her. For the millionth time since finding Lula outside the store, Skye was curious if the sweet-faced baby missed her mother. Did she wonder where she'd gone and why she was with Skye? She shook off the question, knowing that there was no point in dwelling on such things. She believed in Lula's future. If there was anything she could do to ensure her happiness, Skye would do it.

Skye had figured out a way to keep Lula close while still managing to perform tasks around the store. Molly had suggested using the baby sling to keep Lula content while she worked. So far it was working out perfectly. Skye thought Lula enjoyed the close contact between them and the cocoon aspect of the sling. According to the research she'd done online, babies found such spaces comforting.

She began humming an upbeat tune as she set up a new window display featuring a winter wonderland complete with replicas of birch trees and snow. Other than her family's home and the surrounding property, there weren't many places where Skye felt completely at home. Sugar's Place was a haven for her. It always brought her mother to mind, reminding her that Sugar Drummond was still in their hearts and minds. She still lived on through her family.

Skye had spent the last few days trying not to think about Ryan's none too subtle warning about the baby. His meaning had been crystal clear. Don't get too attached.

Too late, a voice buzzed in her ear. Even now she couldn't imagine her life without this little charmer. Lula had quickly burrowed her way into Skye's heart. Although caring for an infant wasn't easy by any means, she found that the daily routine suited her. Diaper changes. Playtime. Bottle feedings. Bath time. Despite the fatigue, Skye felt as if she was doing exactly what she was meant to be doing. God had a plan for her and she was following the path He had laid out for her.

The tinkling sound of the bell above the door heralded the arrival of a customer. Skye warmly greeted the woman, whom she vaguely remembered meeting last year. Darcy? Denise? Something with a *D*. She and her husband had relocated to Serenity Peak from Palmer a year ago. She couldn't recall the woman ever visiting Sugar's Place before.

"Good afternoon. Welcome to the shop," Skye said, extending the customer a warm welcome.

"Hi there," the woman said, waving at her from across the store. "I don't know if you remember me. My name is Deidre Simms." *Deidre!* That was it.

With light brown hair and mahogany-colored eyes, Deidre was an attractive woman. However, Skye sensed a sadness hovering around her like a shadow.

"Yes. We met at the choir concert at Serenity Peak church if I'm remembering correctly," Skye said. "Your husband is Neal, right?"

"That's right," Deidre said. "I joined the choir

a few weeks later because I enjoyed the event so much."

Deidre was a member of the woman's choir. Skye's thoughts immediately went to the button Ryan had found outside the store. So far it was the only clue to Lula's parentage. Did Deidre know something about that? Or had she come to dig around?

"Well, let me know if you have any questions about the merchandise. I'll be right over here setting up the display," Skye explained. Although putting up the display window was one of Skye's favorite tasks, she couldn't help but feel distracted by Deidre's presence.

As the woman roamed around the shop, she kept darting furtive glances at Skye and Lula. Each time Deidre caught her looking, she ducked her head down or focused on something else. Skye had the oddest sensation that there was something Deidre wanted to say to her. She didn't know if her imagination was working overtime, but Deidre's gaze seemed focused on Lula.

When Deidre finally came up to the counter with a basket full of items to purchase, Skye once again noticed her eyes were drawn to the baby.

"She's such a sweet girl," Deidre murmured as she gazed at Lula.

"I don't have a single complaint," Skye said, keeping her tone light. There was no reason for her imagination to run wild or to be on edge. Deidre was harmless.

"I—I heard about you finding Lula outside on the porch," Deidre said. "God works in mysterious ways."

All of a sudden the hairs on the back of Skye's neck were standing at full attention. How did she know Lula's name? She hadn't ever seen Deidre at Sugar's Place before but now she had shown up full of interest in Lula and asking questions. It was giving off red flags.

"Yes, I'm fostering her," Skye explained as she processed Deidre's credit card and bagged up her items. A part of her simply wanted the woman to leave, although she knew it was an uncharitable thought. Skye handed Deidre a sack with Sugar Works's logo printed on the cotton fabric.

"What a blessing," Deidre said as she took her purchases. Her face crumpled and she let out a little cry before heading toward the door.

"Deidre. Is everything all right?" Skye asked as she came from behind the counter.

Deidre turned back to face her with tears streaming down her face. "Not really. I apologize for staring at Lula." She let out a whimper. "My husband and I have been trying for a baby going on two years. We've endured several miscarriages. It's so hard to want to build a family with all of our hearts, only to have those hopes dashed month after month." The tears continued to flow.

The woman's heartbreak was palpable. Skye reached out and placed an arm around Deidre. "I'm so sorry to hear this. I can't imagine how agonizing it's been for you and Neal."

Deidre shook her head. "I don't understand how someone could just abandon their child. Some of us would give the world to be able to call a baby our own."

Skye sucked in a ragged breath. She could see Deidre was hurting, but her comment was harsh. Much like her own words had been upon finding Lula, if she was being honest. Now she didn't feel comfortable downing Lula's mother. Her feelings had changed so much in such a short time. There were still so many unknowns about the situation. She couldn't imagine anyone would easily relinquish a baby. In her opinion it was an act of courage and not a moral failure.

"Sometimes, Deidre, people do the best they can, depending on their circumstances," she told Deidre in a gentle voice. "I don't want to judge Lula's mother. I haven't walked in her shoes, so how can I? Judge not, lest ye be judged."

Deidre took a moment before responding. "You're right, Skye. Neal tells me the same thing." She bit her lip. "I've allowed myself to become bitter over my situation. It's wrong to take my disappointment out on someone I don't even know."

"It's understandable," Skye reassured her as she patted her shoulder. "All I can tell you is don't give in to despair. You and Neal will be in my prayers," Skye said. And she meant it.

As more customers filed into the shop, Skye said her goodbyes to Deidre. She watched from the window as the woman walked to her car. Skye hoped things got better for Deidre and that her hopes regarding having a baby were answered. She knew all too well about being at a low point in life and feeling both helpless and hopeless. "This too shall pass," Skye said, wishing she had given Deidre that nugget of advice. Sometimes it was hard to see the sunshine through the shadows, although storms always passed.

Skye's own nerves were clearly fraught with tension and worry. She had totally read the situation with Deidre wrong. The poor woman longed for a baby of her own. For some reason she'd been nervous that Deidre was Lula's mother coming back to lay claim to the baby. It was so strange to feel territorial over Lula, but she couldn't deny these feelings, which made her feel ashamed. Her role in the baby's life was a temporary one, just as Ryan had reminded her. She had no claim on Lula.

As she looked around at the customers perusing merchandise, Skye couldn't help but wonder if Lula's mother was someone she regularly crossed paths with in town or at Sunday service. Why had she been singled out to find Lula? Was it because her family had established themselves in the Serenity Peak community as a foster family? Or had Lula's birth mother made contact with her at some point in time? She had been going over a few employees' names in her head and trying to figure out if it was possible that they could be connected with Lula. So far she hadn't come up with anything substantial. Since she worked at Sugar's Place, Skye didn't always see the employees who were working with Violet and her dad at Sugar Works. She had no idea if someone had been carrying a child or concealing a pregnancy. There were so many possibilities.

With every passing day her questions continued to mount. She was beginning to wonder if she would ever get any real answers about Lula's origins.

Ryan stood up from his desk and stretched his arms above his head. He had been sitting down for way too long and now he needed to walk off some energy. Maybe he should head over to Northern Lights to grab a sandwich or a salmon burger. Truth be told, his stomach had been making grumbling sounds for the last hour.

Just as he was about to head out the door, Gideon called him into his office. His boss didn't waste any time getting down to business.

"How are things going with Skye and the baby? I know that you've been checking in on them as I requested." Gideon tried to hide it, but he was a big soft teddy bear underneath his gruff demeanor. Ryan knew he was deeply invested in Lula's case. Lately, Gideon had babies on the brain since he and his wife, Sadie, were expecting their first child.

Ryan felt the corners of his mouth relax into a wide grin. "Lula's doing really well. Skye has taken to fostering like a duck to water. She's a natural." Thoughts of Skye snuggling Lula against her chest caused a heartwarming sensation to envelop him.

Gideon took a lengthy sip of his coffee before asking, "Do you have any leads on her parents? There's some pressure on us to get answers."

"I might," he admitted. "I found a button at Sugar's Place that can be traced back to the women's choir at Serenity Church. I'm planning to go over there and talk to some of the group."

His shoulders sagged. "That doesn't give you much to go on," Gideon pointed out.

"Well, maybe it does. I arrived at Sugar's Place shortly after Skye discovered Lula. When I found the button, it was sitting on the top layer of freshly fallen snow. I think it could be a piece to the puzzle because no one but Skye had been out there until I arrived."

"Good points," Gideon said with a nod. "Sounds like you have a place to start."

Ryan leaned against the doorjamb and folded his arms across his chest. "I just want to make sure we're not violating any safe haven laws by investigating," Ryan said. He knew that Alaska offered protection to individuals surrendering their babies under certain conditions.

"Alaska's safe haven law only applies to babies under twenty-one days. Also, Sugar's Place isn't listed as a Safe Haven location." He shrugged. "So we're duty bound to dig into this one."

He nodded. Every day as a state trooper he learned something new and invaluable that helped him perform his job. In that he had never investigated an abandoned baby before, there was a sharp learning curve. He liked the way Gideon always treated him like an equal rather than a newbie.

"I sense that Lula's parent or parents had good intentions. Someone clearly left the baby so Skye would find her. She's had that morning schedule for months now."

"It sure looks like it since she opens up the shop most mornings," Gideon said. "That shows discernment, but we still need answers. We need to follow any clues we can to resolve this."

Ryan scratched his jaw. "I'll do my best." He was still proving himself as a state trooper, so solving this case would be big for him. Because of his past, Ryan felt grateful that he had been given this opportunity. Despite his wild child days, Ryan had never been arrested, which had allowed him to pursue his law enforcement goals.

"Let's keep a lid on this investigation. Everyone in town is buzzing about the baby being left at Sugar's Place. You know what that means." Gideon wiggled his eyebrows.

"Yep. Lots of speculation and whispers." He knew the drill in small towns like Serenity Peak. This story would be fodder for everyone in town for the foreseeable future.

Gideon let out a groan. "And pretty soon there'll be finger-pointing. It could get quite messy, not to mention ugly."

He really didn't want to see anyone else endure the town rumor mill like his own family had.

"The faster we can resolve things, the better. I should get right on it and head over to the church to do some digging," Ryan said.

"That sounds good." His boss locked eyes with Ryan. "Please don't pass anything on to Skye about the investigation." He held up his hands. "I'm not trying to question your professionalism, but I know Skye can be a very persuasive young lady. She's a beautiful woman who's been through a lot." He tapped his finger to his chin. "I seem to recall you having a crush on her a while back."

Ryan shook his head. "That's not going to happen. I would never compromise an investigation," he said. "I did show her the button I found, but I had to in order to eliminate it belonging to her or Violet." And it had been a wise move, since Skye recognized the button from the choir cloak.

He was a little bit salty that Gideon thought for a single second he needed to caution him. Ryan wouldn't address his boss's comment about his feelings for Skye. Clearly, Gideon had a memory like an elephant. Ryan didn't even remember telling him anything about his teenage feelings for her, so maybe he'd simply picked up on it over the years. At this point they were dead and buried, so it was a moot point as far as he was concerned.

"I appreciate you, Ryan. Let me know if you need anything," Gideon said. Ryan said goodbye and headed out the door.

Gideon's parting words instantly soothed his ruffled feathers. For someone who hadn't heard good things about himself for years, it meant the world to him. And he wouldn't forget his sacred duty as a trooper. Loyalty. Integrity. Courage.

Within minutes of getting in his vehicle, Ryan had arrived at Serenity Church. He knew from the church's online schedule that choir practice would be concluding soon. Maybe, if things aligned perfectly, he would be able to talk to some of the members.

Tread carefully, he reminded himself as he pulled open the beautiful oak doors. He loved being at this place of worship. Now that he had renewed his faith, he appreciated being in this sacred place all the more. The sounds of voices raised in song immediately reached his ears. He walked a few feet and sat down in a pew at the back of the church. He was treated to a melodic medley of spiritual hymns.

As practice ended, he spotted Autumn, his uncle Judah's wife, walking toward him. With her warm brown skin and chiseled features, she was a striking woman. He couldn't be happier about her and Judah reuniting after more than a decade apart. They were a strong, inspiring love match.

"You ladies sounded wonderful," Ryan said, wishing he'd been able to listen for longer. Music had always been soothing to his soul. How many times had he attended service with his mother and enjoyed the choir's melodies?

"Thank you, Ryan," Autumn said as she leaned in for a hug. "Singing is a nice outlet for me, especially as a new mother. I recently joined the group. So far it's been a lot of fun." She looked over at a few women who were huddled together, talking in an animated manner. "Everyone is a little on edge today."

"Really? What's going on?" He discreetly turned his head, following the direction of Autumn's gaze. From this distance he couldn't make out the identities of all three women, but he knew one was Gracelyn Handel, a former classmate of his. Although he'd always thought of her as calm and collected, at the moment she seemed quite upset. She was speaking in a raised voice and waving her arms around. He couldn't quite make out what she was saying.

Autumn made a face. "I'm not sure, but there's been a lot of tension and loud whispers. You could cut it with a knife all during rehearsal."

"Is that unusual?" he asked, trying not to be too obvious in his probing.

Autumn narrowed her gaze as she stared at him. She put her hand on her hip. "Ryan Campbell. I've known you since you were a baby. What gives?"

"What are you talking about?" he asked in his most neutral voice. As a journalist, Autumn had a tendency to ferret out information like a blood-hound. Last year she had done major investigative work on fraud in the fishing industry, and shone a spotlight on illegal activities. Putting one over on Autumn would be near impossible.

"Are you here in an official capacity?" she asked, her brow furrowed.

"I cannot confirm or deny that," he said. "If I did, Gideon would call me on the carpet."

She let out a gasp. "Is this about the baby Skye is fostering? "Do you think the child is linked with the women's choir in some way?"

Ryan let out a groan. "Autumn, please don't ask me questions I'm not at liberty to answer. We may be family, but I've got to remain professional."

She shot him a pointed look. "Okay, I understand, but your mere presence here is going to raise some eyebrows. It's not every day that a state trooper shows up for choir practice, especially on the heels of a baby being mysteriously left at Sugar's Place."

Autumn was right. Showing up at Serenity Church was as subtle as a sledgehammer. But maybe it would rattle someone enough so that the truth would come to the forefront.

Just as he was about to respond to Autumn, the

three women walked by, and they all exchanged greetings with him. As Gracelyn passed by him, Ryan glanced at her cloak. He had to mask his emotions. Unlike the cloaks worn by the other women, Gracelyn's was missing a button at the neckline.

Chapter Seven

"I know, sweetheart," Skye crooned in a sing-song voice as she patted Lula's back. "I know you're not feeling well."

Lula responded by letting out a heart-wrenching cry.

Skye wasn't sure she had ever known true exhaustion until this very moment. The last twenty-four hours had been filled with nonstop crying from Lula. She didn't have a fever. She was properly hydrated and wetting diapers. And she had an appetite. For the life of her, Skye couldn't figure out what was going on. On the whole, Lula was an even-tempered baby who rarely fussed. All of a sudden, she was inconsolable.

Although Skye wasn't a baby expert, she knew something wasn't right. But what?

Last night her sister had pitched in to help out, walking up and down the halls with Lula on her hip. The baby had finally fallen asleep with exhaustion, but after a few hours the crying had started up again. Skye was at her wits' end. She hated to see Lula suffering and it made her feel as if she wasn't equipped to be her caretaker. Had she taken on too big a responsibility by offering to foster Lula?

Lord, please help this little girl. Please give me the strength and discernment to make it through this moment. Grant me the wisdom to figure out what's wrong.

She reached for her cell phone and texted Violet. Lula won't stop crying. HELP.

At the moment, Violet and her father were out on the property dealing with some diseased birch trees. She only reached out to them for emergencies, and even though the situation was distressing she couldn't justify calling them out in the field for a crying child. The text would have to do for now. But what if it *was* an emergency? What if it was Lula's appendix or colic? She should call Poppy and take her over to the clinic. Even if it was a false alarm she would feel better getting reassurance from a physician.

A sudden knock on the front door provided a distraction from Lula's ear-splitting cries. She placed Lula in the baby swing and gently pushed it, hoping to soothe her. "I'll be right back," she said in a gentle voice. Regardless of her own fears, she needed to project a calm demeanor.

Babies picked up on the energy of their caretakers. If she was upset, Lula would know.

"You've got this," she reminded herself as walked toward the front door and pulled it open.

"Ryan!" Relief washed over her at the sight of him standing on the threshold.

Even though she had initially been annoyed at the idea of Ryan showing up periodically to check in on her and Lula, she had to resist the urge to hug him for appearing at her doorstep in a moment of crisis.

He was holding a box of cider doughnuts in his hands. Her stomach lurched with hunger. She hadn't eaten since last night. "I hope I'm not disturbing you. It's not nap time is it?"

Skye ran a shaky hand through her hair. "Nap time. I wish. What's that?"

Ryan frowned as he studied her expression. "You seem rattled. Is everything all right?"

She beckoned him inside, then led him toward the kitchen. Lula was sitting in the swing, wailing. Skye threw up her hands. Even the back-and-forth motion of the swing wasn't working to cease the infant's crying. Normally it worked within minutes. What was going on?

"I'm not sure what's wrong. She's been crying since yesterday. She was up for most of the night, fussy and upset," Skye explained. Even though she wanted to appear strong in front of Ryan, she wasn't sure how long she could maintain her composure. "You have no idea how many ways I tried to settle her down. Music. A bottle. Jostling her on my hip. Walking the hallways." Skye let out an agonized groan. "Nothing seems to work."

"It sounds stressful," Ryan said, watching as she lifted Lula from the swing and perched her on her hip. "No offense, but you look wiped out."

"None taken," she said, smoothing back her hair. She should have taken a brush to her hair this morning, but as it was she'd barely had enough wherewithal to brush her teeth and get dressed. "I would feel so much better if a doctor looked her over. I'll never forgive myself if something's really wrong with her and I didn't consult a professional. Am I overreacting?"

Ryan could easily see the distress etched on Skye's beautiful face. Even with dark shadows resting underneath her eyes, she was stunning. He could see that her imagination was running wild with dire scenarios. He had no idea how to make things better, but he was going to use all the skills he'd learned as a trooper to try his best.

"Okay. Take a deep breath," he said in his most calming voice. He demonstrated by taking a big breath of his own. He had seen something similar with his baby cousin, River, and he had a feeling it might be the same issue.

Skye slowly inhaled, closing her eyes. After a few seconds she opened them and exhaled.

"Let's not call Poppy just yet. I have an idea," Ryan said, turning toward the sink to wash his hands. When he was done he moved back toward Skye.

"I just want to check something out. Can you hold Lula tightly against your chest while I look inside her mouth?"

"Of course. At this point I'm anxious to make things better," Skye said, firmly holding the baby in her grasp. He couldn't help but notice she was trembling. Seeing her so helpless caused his heart to seize up. He would give anything to allay her fears.

Ryan took his finger and placed it on Lula's gum line. He immediately felt a little protrusion. "Aha. I think that I found the culprit. She's cutting her first tooth."

"A tooth? That's what's going on?" she asked, her face crumpling.

"Yep. I can feel it almost breaking through the surface. It won't be long now till the tooth shows up and then I'm guessing she'll feel much better. If you gently massage the area, she's going to get some relief." That was the case for River, anyway. He was hoping his words would be a balm for Skye, but from the looks of it, she wasn't feeling very reassured. "You don't look relieved.

What's going on? I thought you would be over the moon."

"I should have known that she was teething. Why didn't I figure it out on my own?" she asked, still sounding upset. She began to massage the area where the tooth was cutting through the gum. Lula responded by gurgling.

"It's okay, Skye. You're human. Give yourself a break. I only thought of it because I remember Autumn and Judah's son River going through it recently." He reached out and placed his hand on her shoulder, then pulled her against his side. Although he wasn't sure if he was overstepping, she sank against him.

Tears slid down her face. "I'm no good at this! I couldn't even figure out that she's teething and yet you put all the pieces together in an instant. What does that say about my mothering skills?"

"Hey, don't cry. You're going to upset Lula." He reached out and wiped her tears away with his thumb. He was standing so close to her he could see droplets on her inky black lashes and tiny freckles scattered on her cheeks. Skye quieted down, although she was still trembling and the tears hadn't stopped flowing. "Don't beat yourself up over it," he said. "You're just exhausted and worried and frustrated. It's understandable. If it means anything, I think you're doing an amazing job."

A hint of a smile played around her lips. "That means a lot to me. I haven't wanted to succeed at anything more in my life. Lula deserves the best."

"You *are* the best." He grinned at her. "You're a natural."

"Thanks, Ryan. Again, it means a lot."

When she turned the full force of her smile on him it was almost blinding. For a moment he was so taken aback by the way it made him feel that he was speechless. His chest tightened and his knees felt a bit wobbly. This was reminiscent of the way she'd made him feel back in high school. Thankfully, he had moved on since those days. He no longer harbored any romantic illusions about Skye. He was happy to simply be her friend and lend support with her foster child.

"Do you have any large carrots?" he asked, turning his attention back to Lula's teething issue.

She knit her brows together. "I think so. Why?"

"Another tidbit I learned from Autumn. Letting a baby suck on a carrot eases teething discomfort. Using a bigger one is safer due to choking hazards."

Skye handed Lula to him and turned toward the fridge. After rummaging around for a few seconds she turned back toward him holding up a carrot. "Ta-da! I found one." She rinsed it off in the sink and placed it in Lula's mouth. The baby grabbed ahold of it and began vigorously sucking on it. Ryan and Skye exchanged a knowing glance.

"I can't believe it! She's happier than I've seen her all day," Skye said, chuckling. "Thanks for the save."

"You can give Autumn the credit," Ryan said. "That woman is a fountain of baby information." He placed the baby down in her high chair. For the moment, Lula was content.

"Well, something tells me you're going to be a fantastic dad one day. You're calm under pressure and very compassionate."

"I get it from my dad," Ryan said as a feeling of pride spread across his chest. "He's the best father and friend I could ever ask for. There hasn't been a single time that he's let me down when I needed him. I'm blessed."

Skye nodded. "I feel the same way about my dad. He went through the heartache of losing my mother, the love of his life, after she passed from the flu." Her eyes moistened. "Nothing could ever prepare someone for that type of devastating loss, yet he never wavered in raising me and supporting Violet. He's one amazing man."

He ran a hand over his jaw. They had both been extremely fortunate to have been raised by men like Abel and Leif—strong, moral, family men. He wanted to be that kind of man and he was working toward that goal one day at a time.

"I can't tell you how grateful I am for your help today, especially after I've had such an attitude with you." Skye let out a sigh. "I've been out of sorts for a long time. I really started to doubt myself when things fell apart in my personal life. It's sad that Tyler's decision not to get married made me feel as if I didn't have anything to offer. I feel embarrassed admitting that but it's true."

He let out a brittle laugh. "You don't have to be ashamed for feeling that way. I know exactly what you mean. For a long time, I let a lot of folks down." He winced as painful memories came to the forefront. "Especially my dad. I was drinking too much and running around with guys who said they were my friends but really couldn't care less about me." He blew out a huff of air. "I was courting way too much trouble."

"And with a different girl every week?" she asked with a slight smirk.

"Yes," he admitted. "I was very immature in my thinking. And my actions reflected that. My dad has been a great influence in leading me back to my faith. That's been a huge path forward for me."

"We all make mistakes and we're all sinners, Ryan. That's a fact," Skye said.

His face flushed at the remembrance of how he'd led his life. "I'm not proud of the way I acted up, but I was mourning the loss of so many things. Zane, Aunt Mary...and then my mom divorced my dad and left us both behind. She's started a new life in Anchorage that doesn't include me. She's engaged to this other guy and I think I'm just a reminder of her past." His throat felt like sandpaper as he made the confession. Talking about his mother, Deborah, always made him feel vulnerable. Even though he wasn't a kid any longer, being estranged from her was still incredibly painful.

Skye let out a sympathetic sound, then reached out and clasped his hand in hers, giving it a comforting squeeze. "It's so hard when it feels as if everything in your life is slipping away from you, isn't it?"

He nodded, not trusting himself to speak past the huge lump in his throat. Ryan hated being emotional about his mother, but the current situation was hurtful. He hadn't seen her in more than six months and their contact had been limited since she'd left town. There was a little part of him that had hoped she'd return to Serenity Peak once he made something of himself by becoming a state trooper. So far her silence spoke volumes.

"I remember your mom coming to all the school performances when we were small. Her love for you was so big it bounced off the walls. Circumstances may have changed, but I don't think her love for you has gone away. Maybe just give her some time to sort herself out."

"That's what my dad thinks as well. He keeps reminding me that this is about her and not me. I appreciate you reminding me of that."

They were standing so close to each other with their hands joined and their arms touching. It felt intimate in a way he'd never experienced with Skye before. After so many years of her being upset with him due to a misunderstanding, it was nice to be in a better place with her. He valued her friendship.

The sound of footsteps drew them apart just as Violet appeared in the doorway.

"Hey! I came as soon as I saw your message," Violet said, stopping when she saw them. She was looking at them with wide eyes, as if she was surprised by seeing them together. Ryan hoped she hadn't misinterpreted their close proximity for anything romantic. The townsfolk tended to pair him up anytime he spent time with a woman. He couldn't say he blamed them considering his track record, but he and Skye had always been just friends.

"What was the emergency?" Violet asked, her gaze still darting between them. Lula had quieted down considerably since she had the carrot to soothe her gums.

A sheepish expression sat on Skye's face. "It seems ridiculous now but Lula has been crying nonstop all day, just like yesterday. I was getting really concerned until Ryan came and saved the day."

Ryan scoffed. "You're giving me way too much credit. You would have figured it out." He reached out and grazed Lula's cheeks with his knuckles. "I'm just happy she's happy now."

"I know. I'm not sure I'll ever get used to hearing her sobbing," Skye said, wrinkling her nose. "It really tugged at my heartstrings."

"Well, I'd better head back to the office," Ryan said, shifting from one foot to the other.

For the life of him, he couldn't figure out why Violet was boring a hole straight through him. Perhaps she really did think there was something going on between him and Skye. The mere thought of it made him want to laugh out loud. He still wasn't sure whether or not Skye could tolerate him as a friend.

Little did Violet know, he couldn't ever view Skye in any romantic way. In his mind she was still Tyler's girl. Off-limits. Out of the question. Not to mention his investigation into the identity of Lula's birth mother. Getting involved with Skye would be blurring the lines between work and his personal life. Being a state trooper was the light at the end of a dark tunnel. For so many years he'd been lost, consumed by a reckless lifestyle and the trauma of losing family members to death and desertion. It was important for him to keep his eye on the prize and not allow anything or anyone to interfere with his career ambitions.

He had worked too hard to get here to mess it all up now.

Violet's gaze trailed after Ryan as he excused himself and headed toward the front door.

"What was that all about? Looks like I interrupted something." She had her hands crossed in front of her and tapped her foot on the kitchen's hardwood floor.

Skye wagged her finger at Violet. "You've been tapping birch trees for too long. You're getting loopy. Ryan and I are just friends."

"I thought you couldn't stand him," Violet countered, smirking. "He appears to have won you over."

Those misplaced emotions seemed like ancient history to Skye. Now at least they were rebuilding a friendship and working together in Lula's best interest. It felt nice to have a burden lifted off her shoulders. She didn't like holding on to anger.

"That was before Lula came along," she explained. "And it was all a misunderstanding based on something Tyler told me. I should have known he wasn't being truthful." At moments like this she really couldn't remember why she'd ever wanted to marry him. It would have been disastrous.

Violet let out an indelicate snort. "That doesn't shock me at all."

Violet's expression said everything. She wasn't a member of her ex-fiancé's fan club.

"You never did like him, did you?" Skye asked. She had never directly asked Violet the question until this very moment.

Violet sank down into one of the dining chairs. "I just didn't think he was a good match for you. You're one of the kindest, most loyal people I've ever known. He was vain and self-centered. To be honest, I could picture you with someone like Ryan."

"But not Ryan himself, since we're just friends," Skye reiterated. What would it take for Violet to get the message? She and Ryan weren't ever going to be an item.

Just the thought of putting herself out there again was terrifying. She had just gotten back to a place in her life where she felt whole again.

Violet held up her hands. "Okay, I get it, but you have to admit he's pretty easy on the eyes.

With those big baby blues and dark hair, he's an Alaskan hottie."

Skye burst into laughter at the look on Violet's face and the way she'd described Ryan. Pretty soon Violet was chuckling right along with her. They were both in hysterics. Lula sat in her high chair gawking at them with the carrot clutched in her chubby hand. Every time they began to settle down, something set off their laughter again.

At this moment, everything in her world felt almost perfect. But a part of her knew that things in her life never stayed this way for long. There was always a calm before the storm. If she'd learned anything at all over the past few years, it was that she had to batten down the hatches in advance of dark clouds.

There was the possibility that Lula's parents could one day come looking for their daughter. Birth parents had the right to change their minds about relinquishing a child. She shook her head at the thought. There must be a statute of limitations on reclaiming a baby after relinquishing them. There had to be rules.

How could she ever prepare herself for something like that? How would she emotionally handle the situation if it came to pass?

Stop it. She was being fanciful and fearful. She didn't want to live with a spirit of fear hanging like a dark cloud over her. She wasn't going to spend another minute thinking about Lula's birth parents. It was unlikely that they would ever resurface or try to claim Lula. Instead she was going to push those thoughts out of her head and focus on the here and now.

Living in the moment and relishing every single second with her foster baby was the antidote to dread and doubt. So far God had been answering all her prayers about Lula and there was no way she was going to take His blessings for granted.

Chapter Eight

The smell of herbs, spices and baked bread hung in the air, serving as a reminder to Ryan that he hadn't eaten since this morning. He had worked straight through lunch trying to track down anyone who might have seen anything suspicious at Sugar Works the morning Lula was discovered. So far, none of the interviews had yielded any leads, which was frustrating. At the moment he was going to relish being at family dinner with the people he loved the most in this world.

"It's been a long time since we've all been around a dinner table together," Leif announced to his family as he looked around the table. "Son, would you like to say grace?" he asked, turning toward Ryan.

"Of course," Ryan answered, bowing his head as he gave thanks for the meal they were about to receive. "Amen," he said as he concluded the blessing and lifted his head back up.

"What an amazing spread," Judah said as he

helped himself to a serving of rosemary mashed potatoes. "Reminds me of the Sunday dinners Mom used to put on."

"Exactly what I was going for," Leif said with a grin. "It's high time that I got back into the swing of things. For far too long I've allowed life to pass me by. Those days are over. I'm going to embrace every day and move forward."

Leif passed a platter of salmon to Ryan. His uncle Judah had caught the salmon on Kachemak Bay a few days ago. As a fisherman, he always had access to the freshest fish in Serenity Peak. The Campbell family had a legacy as fishermen, going all the way back to his great-grandfather.

Ryan knew his father was referencing the dissolution of his marriage and how he'd hit rock bottom in the aftermath. He was finally getting his life back and Ryan couldn't be prouder of him. Despite still being in love with his ex-wife, Leif had given up on his attempts to save the marriage. Both people had to want to salvage the relationship and his mother had made her position clear. She hadn't wanted to do the hard work necessary to fix things. And it truly was too late now that she was in a new relationship and engaged to be married.

He almost couldn't believe what he was hearing. For the last few years his father had been stuck in a terrible limbo, praying and hoping that his wife would come back and give their marriage a second chance. It had been agonizing for Ryan to watch it all play out, especially since his mother had quickly moved on. Thankfully, in the last few weeks he'd seen signs that Leif was ready to move on with his life. He resisted the urge to stand up and cheer. Although he loved his mother, he wasn't sure he would ever be able to forgive her for what she had put his father through. Or him.

He was thankful to have Uncle Judah and Autumn in his life to show him that lasting love was possible. Ryan still harbored hope that someday he would find his other half. Sometimes he struggled to feel worthy of a happily-ever-after but it didn't stop him from wanting one.

"We heard about all the excitement over at Sugar Works," Judah said, glancing toward Ryan. "I understand you were called out to the scene."

"Yes, Skye discovering the baby on the store's porch was a real shock," Ryan said. "I'll give it to Skye, though. She took to Lula right away, almost as if she'd been training her whole life for that moment." Just thinking about Skye's selflessness caused goosebumps to tickle the back of his neck.

"She's a nurturer," Leif said. "Just like her

mother. Sugar was a wonderful woman. A giver. It's nice to see both Violet and Skye take after her. Violet has raised her boy all by herself and done a wonderful job."

"Sugar thought her girls hung the moon," Judah said with a wistful smile. "Her passing was such a terrible loss for the Drummonds." His uncle had endured his own tragedy, so he clearly empathized with Skye's family.

Ryan remembered Sugar Drummond the same way he recalled the first snow of winter and the taste of cinnamon doughnuts. She had been a gentle and lovely woman with a way of making everyone in her orbit feel special. The type of woman who commanded attention everywhere she went, much like Skye herself.

"What a hard choice someone made about the baby," Autumn said, her voice oozing compassion. "To give up your own flesh and blood must be agonizing. I can't fathom that type of courage."

"Must've been really difficult," Leif said, shaking his head. "I imagine a person might spend many a sleepless night going over that decision in their mind."

"And wondering if they'd done the right thing," Ryan murmured. It was something he'd been thinking about a lot. Did Lula's mother regret giving her baby up? Was he on to something with Gracelyn Handel? The missing button on her cloak gnawed at him. And the tension at Serenity Church. Had someone confronted Gracelyn about their suspicions?

"It's surprising that this happened to the Drummonds once before," Leif remarked. "A baby boy was dropped off at their property."

"I remember that," Autumn said. "Violet and I would babysit him from time to time in order to help out. Little Danny was a sweetheart."

Autumn and Violet had been best friends since childhood. It didn't surprise him that she had been hanging out at Sugar Works and helping her friend with foster baby duties when they were young. The two women had been joined at the hip for most of their lives.

"We don't think the two cases are related," Ryan explained. He'd heard folks gossiping in town about the two babies left at Sugar Works and he wanted to nip any speculation in the bud. "It's more likely that the Drummond family has gained a reputation as a solid foster family over the years, which may have led Lula's mother to entrust her baby to them."

"Makes sense," Judah said. "The Drummonds are good people with oversized hearts. They always go above and beyond. I'm sure Skye will be a wonderful foster mother."

It warmed Ryan's heart to hear his family

speak so well of the Drummonds. Lula's mother had chosen wisely by selecting Sugar's Place as a safe spot to leave her baby.

Autumn gently cleared her throat. "Well, Judah and I have some news we'd like to share with you." She looked over at Judah, who had plucked River out of his high chair and placed him on his lap.

"River is going to be a big brother," Judah announced. As he made the announcement, Judah placed a kiss on his son's forehead.

Leif let out a cry of delight and leaned over to give Autumn a hug. "Congratulations. What an incredible blessing!"

Ryan stood up and walked over to his uncle, clapping him enthusiastically on the shoulder. "Such wonderful news, Uncle Judah. You two are going to have your hands full," he said, chuckling. River was only six months old. "Irish twins, isn't that what they call it?"

"As far as I'm concerned, the more the merrier," Judah answered. "We'll take as many as the good Lord sees fit to give us."

"It's amazing how God listens to our prayers." Tears pooled in Autumn's eyes. "I didn't know if it was possible due to my past history and age. But He showed a way for us to grow our family and we're just so grateful."

Last year Autumn had returned to Serenity

Peak, pregnant and newly divorced. She and Judah had reunited, fallen back in love and gotten married. Although Judah wasn't River's biological father, he was a dad to him in every way that mattered most.

Autumn stood up and walked over to the sideboard table. "So, to celebrate, I made my famous wild berry pie."

"Oh, that's a beauty," Leif gushed, rubbing his stomach. "Be still, my heart."

"This pie is a masterpiece. If you weren't already my wife, I just might propose," Judah teased, soliciting laughter from the group.

"And I would accept," Autumn said, beaming down at her husband. "Coming back home to Serenity Peak was the best decision I've ever made other than marrying you."

If Ryan didn't love them both so much he might feel a bit cranky about their affectionate relationship. As it was, he knew how much they'd fought to be together. They had surmounted numerous obstacles to achieve their happy ending. Their love story was one for the ages and he couldn't be happier for the couple. They were living out their dreams in a big way.

"I think we might have some vanilla ice cream to go with this," Leif said, getting up from the table and returning a few moments later with a pint of vanilla bean ice cream.

As they dug in to dessert, Ryan took River from Judah so his uncle could enjoy the pie without River sticking his hands in it and making a mess. It felt nice to finally hold his little cousin without being afraid of painful memories crashing over him.

"Hey, River," Ryan crooned. "I can't wait to take you sledding when you get a little older. Your dad used to take me all the time."

"He's so comfortable with you," Autumn said. "Every time you're around he just lights up. You know what that means."

Ryan had no clue. "No, I don't. Tell me. What does it mean?"

Autumn's lips twitched with mirth. "That you're a baby magnet. And you're destined to have a houseful of your own little crumb snatchers. So get yourself prepared."

Ryan began to sputter, which sent Leif and Judah into hysterics.

"Slow down, Autumn," Leif advised. "He's got to find a wife first."

Ryan laughed along with his family, but Autumn's words had hit him right in the gut.

Lately he had been thinking about his future and yearning for something solid. Marriage and kids seemed so far away at the moment, yet that was the life he truly wanted. Family. Faith. Abiding love. At times he wondered if it was too much to ask for, but being in the presence of Uncle Judah, Autumn and River made it all seem very possible.

He just had to keep his focus on laying the foundation for his future, one brick at a time. Everything else would fall into place.

After Uncle Judah, Autumn and River headed home, Ryan sat down with his father over piping hot cups of green tea. Their conversation landed on the happy baby news. His father was genuinely delighted for his brother and sister-in-law. Perhaps the shadows of the past were finally making way for sunshine.

"Oh, I almost forgot," Leif said, snapping his fingers. "A letter came for you. I think someone dropped it off, because there's no postage on the envelope." His father stood and retrieved a letter from the counter. He handed Ryan a small white envelope with his name scrawled in cursive. He placed his arm around Ryan. "I've got an early morning tomorrow on the Fishful Thinking with your uncle so I'm going to call it a night."

The Fishful Thinking was Uncle Judah's boat. He was in the commercial fishing business, as well as being a co-owner of Northern Lights. Now that they were back on good terms, his dad was working with his brother. Ryan couldn't be happier about this development. He believed their new working relationship assuaged some of his father's loneliness.

Ryan felt a wide smile stretching from ear to ear. After all their losses, nothing mattered more than family. "That's great to hear. The two of you make an awesome team."

"I'm going to take Lady out before I go to bed. In case I haven't said it lately, I'm proud of you and all you've accomplished in the last few years," Leif said before ushering his elderly poodle outside.

His father's parting remark packed a solid punch. Mere words couldn't express how good it felt to bring pride rather than shame and disappointment. These days he stood a little bit straighter when he walked around town. The work he had done to improve himself was paying off.

Ryan looked at the envelope with curiosity before ripping it open and tugging at the piece of paper inside. He pulled the note out and began to read the words.

Dear Ryan,
I want to thank you for being a part of my baby's journey. I know you're watching over her. I know you came to the church to find me. Please don't try to track me down. Lula is better off without me even though I love

*her very much. I took good care of her for
as long as I could. I wish with all of my
heart that things were different.*

*With gratitude,
Lula's Mother*

Ryan read the note several times, his mind
whirling with questions the more he studied the
message. He couldn't figure out why the woman
had sent the note in the first place. The last line
hinted at regret. He had to wonder if she wanted
to make contact with him for a specific reason
not stated in the note. He imagined she must
have questions about her baby's well-being. Even
if she trusted the Drummonds, a mother would
still have qualms.

"Ryan, is everything all right? You look a bit
rattled." His father had come back inside without him even hearing footsteps. He had been so
engrossed in the note and trying to figure out
the intentions behind it.

"I'm fine, Dad. Just tired," he said, folding the
letter in half and stuffing it back in the envelope.

"If you say so," Leif said, frowning. He glanced
at the letter, his mouth opening as if to say something, but then he closed it. "Night, son."

"Good night, Pops," Ryan said, listening as

his father trudged up the stairs with Lady in his arms.

As well as his father knew him, Ryan sensed he didn't quite believe that everything was fine. In that the letter pertained to an active investigation, he couldn't discuss it, even though he was tempted. His dad was a great sounding board and he would surely impart some of his vast wisdom, but he couldn't break the official rules. Tomorrow he would show the note to Gideon and place it in the case file.

So far he only had this letter, the button from a choir cloak and Autumn's account of tension between the choir members to go on. Honestly, it wasn't much in the way of evidence, but he would have to keep digging and keep an open mind. Although the missing button was pointing in Gracelyn's direction, that wasn't conclusive by any stretch of the imagination. He had hit a brick wall with regards to finding any fingerprints on the button, but perhaps this note would yield some prints.

Please don't try to track me down. The words tugged at his heartstrings. They spoke of fear and desperation. He felt disloyal for thinking it, but would it be so bad if they never uncovered the identity of Lula's mother? Ryan put his head in his hands and let out a groan. He had a job to do, and he couldn't allow sympathy for Skye to override his sense of duty.

He wasn't impartial in this case, not by any means. He'd felt protective of Lula since the day she'd been discovered at Sugar's Place. And his friendship with Skye was getting stronger every day. Although he was pleased that they were rebuilding their childhood bond, he couldn't help but wonder what would happen when it was time for her to say goodbye to Lula.

Skye wasn't sure where to start on her to-do list as she sat down at her desk in the study. She needed to take the steps to become certified as a foster parent and she wanted to get it done as soon as humanly possible. She didn't want to run the risk of Lula being removed from her care due to a technicality. That would be heartbreaking.

The list was as long as her arm. Orientation. Application. Background check. Fingerprinting. Home visit. Training. So much to accomplish! At least her father and Violet were up to date on their certification, so they didn't need to repeat the process. Because she'd been under sixteen when her family had last fostered, her fingerprints hadn't been required. She was trying not to get rattled that it seemed as if she was starting at square one with the certification process.

Her brain was feeling a bit scrambled as she

tried to figure everything out. At least most of these tasks could be accomplished online.

"Take a break, Skye," her father said. He was standing behind her, peering over her shoulder. She was surprised to see him in the middle of the day when he would normally be working on the property.

"Go into town and grab a sandwich at Northern Lights or something," he suggested. "Say hello to Molly at the café or do some window shopping. Whatever your heart desires."

Although a break sounded wonderful, Skye knew she had duties here at the house that centered around Lula. This was the path she'd chosen, so it didn't feel right to shirk her responsibilities.

"I can't. Lula's going to need lunch as soon as she wakes up from her nap and I have to put a load of her clothes in the washing machine." She didn't mention the dozen other chores she needed to do.

She felt his hand on her back. "I've handled my fair share of babies, including you," he said, letting out a deep-throated chuckle. "I'm taking the rest of the day off, so put me to use. Lula knows me, so it's the perfect setup."

Her jaw dropped. Abel was the hardest-working man in town and he never took time off. She knew this was all about supporting her and Lula.

And honestly, she could use the break. Then she could come back to her training with a clear head. Skye jumped up from her seat and turned toward her father, throwing herself against his chest. "Oh, Daddy. Thank you. You're always so good at picking up on my feelings and what I need most of all."

He wrapped her in a tight hug. "Anything for you, sunshine. I admire what you're doing with Lula. Fostering isn't for the faint of heart. And you've risen to the occasion. That's commendable."

"You've shown me the way regarding fostering. It's always been embedded in my heart," she said, pressing her hand against her chest. Receiving kudos from her father made her feel as if she could fly to the moon on wings.

"Get going," he said, making a shooing motion with his hands. "I'll be here with Lula. Don't you worry about a thing."

Skye raced upstairs to change into a pair of dark jeans and a cute pink top. She brushed on a hint of lipstick and mascara, knowing she might run into folks in town who she hadn't seen in a while. She wanted them to know that Skye Drummond was back! She wasn't hiding out any longer out of shame. She would walk into Northern Lights with her head held high, no matter who was in the establishment. This seemed like a monumental milestone to her.

As soon as she got to town, Skye went straight to the restaurant. Once she headed inside, she had a moment of nervousness since she wasn't used to eating alone. *Just breathe. You know this place like the back of your hand, as well as the townsfolk.* She sat down at a booth, and heard someone calling her name. A slight turn of her head and there was Ryan, sitting a few feet away at his own table.

He beckoned her toward him. "Come join me. I just sat down." His invitation was good-natured and sincere. An easy smile lit up his face, show-casing his dimples. He really was all kinds of gorgeous. It was funny how she had known him her entire life, yet she was just beginning to ap-preciate his striking good looks.

Her pulse quickened as she walked over to join him. She couldn't think of a single reason to reject his invitation despite the fact that her palms were moist and her heart was beating faster than usual. She nodded and exchanged pleasantries with several customers as she made her way over to Ryan.

Ryan got to his feet and gestured toward the booth. "Take a seat. I was just looking at the menu and trying to decide. The buffalo tenders are always good."

"Thanks," Skye said as she sat down. Ryan slid the menu over to her and she quickly perused it, deciding on a salmon burger and a bowl of seafood chowder.

Moments later the waitress came and placed two glasses of water in front of them. She took their orders and left.

"Where's your sidekick?" Ryan asked, taking a long sip of his water.

"My dad surprised me by offering to watch Lula while I came into town and grabbed lunch. I've been trying to get myself situated with obtaining my certification and the details are a bit overwhelming." She let out a deep breath.

"You've got this," Ryan said, reaching out and placing his hand on hers. Her skin prickled at the contact.

"Thanks. I appreciate your confidence," Skye said, buoyed by his words of affirmation. She needed to repeat his phrase over and over again when things weighed on her.

"That's really nice of Abel to take over for you," Ryan said. "From what I've seen, you deserve a break. It's clear that you put your heart and soul into Lula, but you need to replenish yourself as well."

"You're right about that, and I'm trying to be mindful about accepting offers of help and self-care," she said. She made a mental reminder to book her pedicure and massage appointment. Violet had given her a gift certificate to a local spa on her last birthday. She was going to follow through and set up the appointment.

"Attagirl," Ryan said. "It will benefit both you and Lula."

"This journey has been full of surprises, most of all within myself," Skye blurted out. She was shocking herself by saying something so personal to Ryan, but these days it seemed as if she was running on pure emotion. Lula brought it out in her.

"How so?" Ryan asked. "I'd love to hear."

"I never imagined that I would feel this way about someone else's baby. After Violet had Chase, she used to tell me that her heart expanded in ways that astounded her. I never knew exactly what she meant."

"Until now."

She bobbed her head. "Sometimes I feel as if my heart is going to crack right down the middle. If something isn't right in Lula's world, then nothing's right in mine. I can't even put a name to it."

"If you ask me, that sounds a lot like motherhood." There was a hint of awe in Ryan's tone, and it made her sit up straighter.

That was what this was. *Motherhood.* Sure, she wasn't Lula's biological mother, and her role was temporary foster mom, but Lula was beginning to feel like her very own child. There was something so incredibly powerful about the bond she was developing with the little girl. It still astounded her that she could feel such immense love and protectiveness. But she did. The feelings flowed through her veins. They were stronger than anything she had ever known or experienced.

By the time the food arrived, Skye was famished. They both dug into their lunch and ate in companionable silence. She looked around the place, noticing a few people staring at their table. Instead of assuming the worst, Skye imagined they were simply curious after not seeing her out and about for a while. A feeling of triumph flooded her. She hadn't let the past keep her from living her life.

"Aurora borealis watch on Saturday. Will I see you there?" Ryan asked, wiping his mouth with a napkin and pushing his plate away.

Skye let out a little squeal. She had completely forgotten about the upcoming event that allowed the townsfolk to get a glimpse of the northern lights while enjoying camaraderie with their neighbors. The lively event had always been one of Skye's favorites even though she had stayed away for the past few years. But things were different this year. *She* was different.

"I'm so excited about going, but it will depend on the weather since I'll be bringing Lula along," Skye explained. Alaskan nights could be bitterly cold and she didn't want to subject Lula to a wintry night. Sometimes it took hours to try and get a glimpse of the aurora borealis. They were quite unpredictable.

"I hope it works out. I would love to see you there," he said. "And Lula too," he quickly added.

She caught his gaze and couldn't look away. Something hovered in the air between them, a kind of electricity that hummed and buzzed. All she knew was that it felt as if there had just been a sudden shift. She couldn't breathe normally. She needed to leave right now.

"Well, I need to run a few errands before I head home," she said, rummaging in her purse for some bills, then plopping them down on the table. "Bye, Ryan. Nice seeing you."

Before he could say anything, Skye was making her way across the dining area. She couldn't help but notice stares and whispers as she walked past several tables. Didn't they ever get tired of gossiping about her?

"Hey, Skye. Thanks for stopping by today," Cici said, patting her on the shoulder as she neared the door. "It's great to see you back in the groove again."

It had been a long time since Skye had been

to town for the sole purpose of a social outing. Usually she was running an errand that only required her to be in town for a short period of time. Now she couldn't manage to shake the feeling of being the subject of whispers. Maybe she was being paranoid based on the past, but she needed to find out what was going on. Were people still speculating about Lula?

"Thanks, Cici." She stepped closer and lowered her voice. "Can I ask you something? Are people still talking about my finding Lula at Sugar's Place?" She looked around again. She wasn't imagining the stares and whispers. They still had their eyes trained on her.

"Honey, people aren't whispering about the baby," Cici said, her hand placed on her hip. "They're flapping their jaws about you and Ryan."

"Me and Ryan?" she asked, bewildered. What in the world was Cici getting at?

"Yep." The woman shook her head. "They're already trying to walk the two of you down the aisle."

Skye sucked in a shocked breath. Once again she was the object of town chatter, this time involving Ryan. She shook her head, her mind refusing to believe what Cici was telling her.

She bristled with annoyance. Why was her name on people's lips? "That's ridiculous! Ryan and I are not a couple. And honestly, we never will be!" she said in a raised voice.

Cici's gaze drifted to a spot over her head, and as Skye turned around, she had a sinking feeling in the pit of her stomach. Ryan was standing behind her, and it couldn't be more obvious that he'd heard every word she had just said.

Chapter Nine

The previous night a wintry storm had blanketed Serenity Peak with a few feet of the fluffy white stuff. Ryan loved snowstorms, even minor ones such as this latest squall. There was nothing more beautiful than freshly fallen snow coating the mountains and the trees. He enjoyed all the activities snow brought—sledding, skiing, snowboarding and snowmachining. He was really looking forward to tonight's aurora borealis watch. For what felt like the hundredth time, he wondered if Skye would make an appearance.

Ryan and I are not a couple. And honestly, we never will be!

Just remembering Skye's harsh words made him cringe. He knew that she hadn't meant for him to overhear her conversation with Cici, but he'd felt incredibly awkward in the aftermath. He couldn't even look her in the eyes. They had both left Northern Lights without exchanging another word between them. He still wasn't sure which one of them had been more embarrassed.

Of course they weren't dating, yet he still felt wounded by her acting as if the idea was as likely as her going to the moon for a lunar landing. He shouldn't feel hurt, but he was. It made him realize that despite the recent thawing in their relationship, she still didn't think well of him. *Ouch!*

He shook off thoughts of the encounter and focused on getting ready for the town event. Although he loved being a state trooper, Ryan relished the opportunity to dress in regular clothes tonight rather than his uniform. He put on a pair of dark cords, a gray sweater and his favorite hunter green parka. By the time he arrived at the lookout spot at Serenity Mountains, a sizable crowd had already gathered.

Ryan was meeting up with his best friends, Brody and Caden. The Locke brothers were fraternal twins. They were quite different in appearance, despite their twin status. Caden was taller, with a more rugged build, while Brody's height hovered at around five-ten. Their warm brown skin tones were their only similarity.

"Hey, stranger," Ryan said as he greeted Brody. "Where have you been hiding?"

"Judah has been keeping me busy on the boat,"

Brody answered, chuckling. "If I didn't love fishing so much, I might pick an easier profession."

As a member of his uncle's crew, Brody woke up early and worked grueling hours out on Kachemak Bay. Brody was hardworking and loyal, which made him one of Judah's favorite workers. Caden was a pilot, having just earned his wings.

"Where's Caden?" Ryan asked, looking around the area. He spotted Autumn and Judah talking to a group of friends across the way and waved at them.

"He had a last-minute gig out of Homer," Brody explained. "He's probably not going to make it back in time."

"I guess we're all busy," Ryan said. He missed the days when they could all hang out together with no heavy obligations in their lives. But that was a part of becoming an adult, of growing up. "We need to make plans to get together, maybe use our snow machines."

Brody's face lit up. "That would be great. It's a plan."

"I'm going to hold you to it," Ryan said, excited about filling his downtime doing sporty activities with lifelong friends. The Locke brothers had always been a good influence on him.

"Seems like a good crowd tonight. Everybody's here," Brody said, gesturing toward the throng of people standing by food trucks. The heady aroma of fried fish and tacos drifted to Ryan's nostrils. It was heartwarming to see kids lined up to order hot chocolate and jumping up and down with excitement. Expectation hung in the air at the notion of seeing something spectacular.

"There are the Drummonds," Brody announced. "I heard Tyler might show up, so I hope Skye isn't bothered by his presence."

According to Skye she had moved past her relationship with her ex, so Ryan didn't anticipate any issues. He spotted Skye easily in her bright pink parka, standing with Violet, Abel, Chase and Molly. Lula was bundled up in her arms. Skye made eye contact with him and waved. He nodded in her direction but made no move to walk over. Ever since their awkward moment at the restaurant, he'd been giving her a bit of space. He missed his check-ins with her and Lula, and he needed to get back over to the Drummond home to satisfy Gideon's requirements.

The mood was jovial and upbeat. Everyone was smiling and laughing, which was why he loved this event so much. At least for this moment in time folks were able to put their worries aside and enjoy the feel-good aspect of the night. As a child he had attended this very same event with his own family. Everything had been so simple back then, when his parents had been a happy couple. But maybe he hadn't seen the cracks in their marriage since he'd just been a kid.

He walked over to chat with Gideon and Sadie, marveling at how relaxed his boss seemed in the presence of his wife. Sadie was a lovely woman who had brought so much happiness into Gideon's life. Ryan would eagerly embrace that sort of good fortune for himself.

What would it be like, he wondered, to walk through life with a loving partner by your side? More and more he was asking himself that question and coming up empty-handed each time. Sometimes he thought he was ready to take on love and the joys of marriage and fatherhood, but his past was littered with failed romances. Did he have what it took to go the distance with someone? Stay the course? Focusing on being a state trooper seemed to be the reasonable choice at the moment. At least he knew it was something he was good at.

Suddenly, he felt a tugging sensation on his sleeve. When he turned around, Skye was standing there with bright eyes and a cheerful expression. Just seeing her so close did something funny to his insides. As always she looked radiant with her flawless features and blond hair cascading down her back. A jaunty pink beret sat perched on her head.

"Hey, Ryan. It's nice to see you," she said, a smile playing around her lips. She genuinely seemed sincere, which confused him all the more. He hadn't gotten the best impression the other day at Northern Lights. Perhaps he was being too sensitive.

"Hi, Skye. I'm glad you decided to come out tonight." He looked over at Violet, who was holding the baby. "I see you've got plenty of reinforcements."

"As they say, it takes a village," Skye said, chuckling. "I'm all for that. It's really nice knowing I have backup if I need it."

"That's why family is so important," Ryan said. "I can tell yours loves you a lot."

Skye's expression turned thoughtful. "I don't know what I'd do without them. They're everything to me, especially after losing my mother."

He nodded. "I understand that type of loss. My mother is still living but she's not in my life and there's a huge hole where she used to be," Ryan explained, his voice catching as he spoke. "You're fortunate."

A few seconds of silence passed before Skye said, "It feels like you've been avoiding me." She was chewing on her lip. "You haven't come by the house for days."

"Not at all," he said. "I've just been busy. Gideon keeps me on my toes. In addition to Lula's case I have several others that require my attention." Even though he could have made time to swing by the Drummond home, he'd wanted to give her some distance.

Skye began to wring her mittened hands. "I'm so sorry about the other day at Northern Lights," she said. "I didn't mean to sound so awful." A look of regret was etched on her face.

He waved his hand at her. "No need to apologize. You were just being honest."

She reached out and grasped his arm. "That's not it. I was just frustrated that folks were talking about me all over again." She winced. "It reminded me way too much of all the gossip after the wedding that wasn't. That really did a number on me. Everywhere I turned folks were coming up with a new reason that Tyler called off the wedding. In every version I was to blame. After a while I decided to keep a low profile at home."

Ryan hadn't known things had gotten that bad. "That's awful. I did hear a few stories, but I never imagined how out of control things were back then." Every time he'd heard folks spreading gossip about Skye he'd called them on it. In his own way he'd had Skye's back.

No wonder she had kept a low profile at her family's property. She had been mourning the loss of a life she'd dreamed of and then been scapegoated for her ex's decision. It must have been agonizing.

"I'm so sorry you went through all that. It never makes sense to me how good people can behave so badly," Ryan said, shaking his head. "Gossip like that is so damaging."

"I've put most of that mess behind me, but every now and then something happens to bring it all back. Like the other day at Northern Lights." She wrinkled her nose. "I do think that going through something so awful made me stronger. It strengthened my faith as well. Sometimes it was just me and God. He gave me the will to push through adversity."

"I know what you mean," Ryan said. "I went through some bad times," he admitted, "but when I decided to turn my life around, God walked the walk with me. I'm not sure that I could have changed everything without Him."

Skye was so easy to talk to, he realized. He didn't usually make himself vulnerable to people, but with her it felt different. Effortless. They had a lot in common and they had both relied on their faith in tough times. He had no clue as to how Tyler could ever have let such a good woman go.

"By the way, you were right," she announced, bowing her head.

He knit his brows together. "About what?"

She looked up, moisture pooling in her eyes. "About my getting too attached to Lula." She looked away from him. Her voice was shaking. "I'm in really deep, Ryan. And I'm not sure how to get myself out."

There! She had admitted to someone that Lula's presence in her life was getting complicated. And Ryan of all people was the person she had chosen to unload on. As much as she adored Lula, the little charmer was now indelibly imprinted on her heart. She had to acknowledge that getting her feelings off her chest felt good. Relief swept through her.

A look of confusion came over Ryan's face. "What exactly do you mean?"

She let out a little sigh. "I love Lula with all my heart. Utterly and completely. And I can't imagine my life without her. Don't you see? That's the problem." Skye wrapped her arms around her middle. "I don't want to sound selfish because her well-being is the most important thing of all. And I know that. If a family wants to adopt her, I need to embrace that reality and do everything I can to support them."

"But?" Ryan asked, his brows furrowed. "I can hear a *but* coming."

"I think it's going to be a heartbreak for me

when she leaves," she let out. Again, her heart constricted and she felt as if she couldn't breathe properly. "I'm not sure if I can handle another heartache."

"Skye, you're going to be fine. I think you feel so attached to Lula because you were the one who found her. And it's reasonable to think that you were chosen to be that person by her mother. That knowledge is powerful. It would be strange if you didn't feel this type of connection."

"Do you really think so?" she asked. "I'm not overdoing it?" Sometimes she wondered if Lula was filling up this lonely ache inside of her.

"I think you care about Lula. You love her. And that's what we're here to do. Love one another," Ryan said, his voice sounding sure and strong. "How can that be a bad thing?"

The new and improved Ryan Campbell was constantly surprising her. He was wise and sensitive. And he listened without judgment.

"Don't take this the wrong way, but you've changed a lot," Skye said. "Not that you weren't a good guy before, but you're different now."

"Maybe you just weren't looking closely enough," he said in a teasing tone that made her laugh.

Although she knew he was joking, Ryan was right. She had been so wrapped up in her ex that she hadn't been able to see straight. Suddenly, it felt as if she was viewing life with a new pair of glasses. Everything in her world was now in vivid color. It was a thrilling feeling!

Just then Violet walked up with Lula in her arms bundled in a thick blanket. "Hi there, Ryan," she said warmly. "It's a beautiful night we're having, isn't it?"

"Hey, Violet. It's shaping up to be a perfect night for watching the northern lights." He reached out and swept his gloved hand across Lula's cheek. "Hey there, cutie," he gushed, eliciting a smile from the baby. Lula clearly recognized Ryan. Her reaction to him was adorable. It seemed she wasn't the only one bonding with Lula. Ryan was making his own impression.

"I was going to head on home and take Lula with me since she's getting sleepy. I've got to head to Palmer in the morning on business," Violet explained.

"Are you sure?" Skye asked. "I can go with you if you like."

"No. You stay and enjoy yourself," Violet said with a shake of her head. "Dad is going to stay, so he can drive you and Chase home. Just keep an eye on my son, please. Between you and Dad being here, he'll be fine. Lula's car seat is in my truck so it all works out perfectly."

"If you're certain," Skye said. Although she was grateful to her sister for making such a kind offer, she couldn't shake the feeling that Lula was her responsibility.

"I'm one hundred percent certain, sis," Violet said with a wave of her hand. "See you in the morning."

Before Skye could change her mind, Violet was walking toward the parking lot with a purposeful stride. She watched as her nephew raced over to give his mother a goodbye kiss. The sweetness of the moment tugged at her heartstrings. The idea of not being able to watch Lula grow up caused tears to pool in her eyes. She blinked them away before Ryan noticed.

What's wrong with me? Her role as a foster mother was bringing out a host of emotions. After stuffing down her feelings over the last few years, everything was suddenly rising to the surface. She was an emotional mess.

"Are you okay?" Ryan asked, peering at her. He really was tuned in to people's emotions, which was an endearing attribute.

"I'm fine. It's just heartwarming seeing Violet and Chase together. It always chokes me up. My sister's been through a lot as a single mother. I admire her so much for the life she's made for him." A little sigh slipped past her lips. "I need to tell her that more often."

"The fact that it's so moving to you speaks volumes. I'm sure Violet would love to hear that type of affirmation from you, especially since she's been doing all the heavy lifting by herself. I think it probably resonates with you more now that you're fostering Lula."

Ryan was right. She now knew firsthand how difficult it was to take care of a child, although Violet had been putting in the hard work for nine years. An idea popped into her head. She would plan a day of relaxation for Violet in recognition of all of the hard work she did working at Sugar Works and being the best mom in the world to Chase.

Suddenly, cries rang out in the crowd as the sky exploded in bursts of reds, greens and purples. Skye cheered in delight as the heavens began an amazing show.

"Oh, it's spectacular," she gushed, tilting her head up toward the sky.

"Let me show you the best vantage point to see the lights. I promise you won't be disappointed." Ryan grabbed her by the hand. Without asking a single question, she trailed after him as they made their way to higher ground.

Once they reached the location, Skye knew exactly why Ryan had led her to this ridge. From this viewpoint it seemed as if she could reach out and touch the sky.

"Ahh. You're a pro at this," she said. This spot provided the perfect vantage of the night sky, far away from any trees or the crowd. Suddenly it felt as if it was just the two of them out here in the quiet watching a magnificent light show in the sky.

"Can you imagine some folks go their entire lives without seeing the aurora borealis?" Ryan asked, shaking his head in amazement. "I've always thought it was lights dancing in the sky."

"I don't think I'll ever get over how lovely this is," she said, gazing upward. She had grown up seeing this stunning sight, yet it never got old. Each time felt like the first time. And tonight, with Ryan by her side, this moment seemed perfect.

"One of the most beautiful sights in Alaska," Ryan said, sounding awestruck as he gazed up at the heavens.

Skye looked over at him. She wasn't looking up at the sky any longer because right now Ryan fascinated her way more than the northern lights. He turned toward her with a look of reverence stamped on his expressive face.

Their faces were so close together, she could see the slight five-o'clock shadow on his jaw and the slight creases by his mouth. The glow from the sky lit up his face so that she could see the brilliance emanating from his eyes. Neither one looked away. She couldn't help but wonder what he was thinking.

"I hope I'm reading this moment right," Ryan said as he leaned over and dipped his head down, pressing his lips over hers. His mouth was warm, and he tasted like hot cocoa or something else sweet. Cinnamon perhaps. Skye leaned into the kiss, placing her arms around Ryan's neck and pulling him closer. As the kiss deepened and soared, Skye steadied herself against the sensation that her legs were giving way beneath her. Ryan's hands wrapped around her waist, steadying her against the sensation of falling.

She hadn't experienced anything quite like this in her life. Maybe it was the aurora borealis, but she felt like fireworks were going off between them.

When they finally pulled apart, she felt the immediate loss of his nearness. She resisted the impulse to pull him back in for another kiss.

"That may have just made this beautiful night all the sweeter," Ryan said, brushing his hand across her cheek.

Just as she opened her mouth to respond, her nephew came running toward them, shouting at the top of his lungs. Skye took a step back. "Auntie Skye! Here you are. We've been looking for you everywhere." Chase wrapped his arms around her waist. "What are you doing way up here?"

"Ryan wanted to show me the best viewing

spot," Skye explained. She pointed up. "It's a pretty amazing view up here."

Chase looked up at the flashing night sky filled with an abundance of brilliant colors. "Wow. This is an awesome spot to watch!" Chase said, his voice filled with awe.

"You can hang out here with us if you like," Ryan suggested, placing his arm around him. "Go get your friends to join you."

"Oh, that's a great idea. I'll be right back," Chase said, running off in the direction he'd come from. Skye wasn't sure he'd ever run so fast in his life.

Skye burst out laughing at Chase's exuberance. "I think you have a fan for life," she said to Ryan. She didn't say it out loud, but she knew Chase was drawn to father figures due to the lack of a father in his life.

"The feeling is mutual. If I had his energy I could move mountains," Ryan said, chuckling. "He's some kind of wonderful."

"That he is," Skye concurred. She appreciated Ryan's kind words about Chase. Although her nephew projected a confident, carefree air, that wasn't always the case. Having a friend like Ryan in his life could only serve to boost his self-esteem. She prayed Ryan would spend more time with him. He'd be around anyway because of Lula.

"He reminds me of Zane," Ryan admitted. She couldn't help but notice a slightly wounded expression on his face.

"I'm sorry. It must be difficult to see so many children running around tonight while still grappling with your own grief." Skye knew from her own experience that grief was open-ended and raw. There was no predicting when it would rise up and grab you by the throat.

"It's funny. I love being around kids. Hearing their laughter makes me feel that all is right with the world. But then I remember that Zane isn't here and that doesn't feel right. He didn't even make it to his ninth birthday, which will never make sense." He let out a ragged sigh. "I ask God all the time why he took Zane and Aunt Mary, but I'm still waiting for an answer."

"I've been in your shoes, Ryan. Losing my mom was a shock for all of us. How could someone so vital and loving be taken from the world?" She blinked back tears. "I think even if we don't get the answers we're seeking, God is listening. He hears us."

Ryan nodded. "Once upon a time I wouldn't have believed that, but I do now. That belief has seen me through a lot of painful times. Without Him in my life I'm not sure that I would've had the strength to reinvent my life and become a state trooper or been able to deal with my mom walking out on us. I'm stronger now than I've ever been."

Moments later Chase returned with a group of friends who were all boisterous and loud.

They watched the rest of the display of lights in the sky as a group, the kids providing additional entertainment with their lively commentary. Skye hadn't laughed so much in years. This was what she needed. Being out in her Alaskan community, surrounded by positivity, was good for the soul. It was good for her.

Dear Lord, I am so grateful for this night and for the stunning skies that You created. I am stronger today than I was yesterday and that is due to Your grace.

Later that night, on the way home, Skye's thoughts turned to Ryan and the kiss they had shared. Neither she nor Ryan had mentioned it when they had said their good-nights to one another.

Although the kiss had made her feel as if she were flying, Skye wasn't sure she should have gone there with Ryan. Their friendship was important to her, and she didn't want to make things complicated. It reminded her of the story about Icarus flying too close to the sun. Even if something made you feel good it didn't mean that it was good for you.

Although she had fallen out of love with Tyler

a long time ago, Skye wasn't sure she was ready to plunge headfirst into another romantic relationship. She had given her all to her relationship with her ex-fiancé and planned out her future with him, yet she'd ended up brokenhearted and betrayed. It was unthinkable to imagine having her heart smashed into a million pieces all over again. She didn't think she was strong enough to take the risk.

Chapter Ten

Seeing the aurora borealis the other night paled in comparison to kissing Skye. Ryan had barely been able to think of anything else in days. The kiss had been out of this world. Tender and powerful. Memorable and potent. He hadn't wanted it to end, yet a part of him had known it wasn't the brightest move he had ever made. For so long he'd thought of her as Tyler's girl, off-limits and out of reach. This sudden shift in their relationship was hard to wrap his head around.

The bottom line was that he shouldn't have let the kiss happen. Ryan considered himself a consummate professional and he was in the middle of a case involving Skye's foster child. The lines were becoming blurred, especially since Lula's mother had reached out to him with that touching letter. Ryan couldn't share that information with Skye, which gnawed at him a little bit. He couldn't shake the feeling that the situation was coming to a head and he would be smack-dab in the middle of the fallout.

The other night he had spotted Gracelyn at the aurora borealis viewing. She'd been staring at Violet when she'd been holding Lula in her arms. Her gaze had been intense and more attentive than a casual observer's might be. After adding up the few clues he had, everything was pointing in her direction as Lula's birth mother. He had confirmed his suspicions by finding out from Autumn that she had been MIA from choir for a number of months this past year, which matched up with the latter parts of a pregnancy and Lula's birth month. At the same time, Ryan couldn't justify interrogating Gracelyn based on the missing button and his suspicions. The note had showed partial fingerprints, but nothing that was in the system was a match.

When he'd arrived at work this morning, Ryan had laid it all out for Gideon.

"It all adds up, but it's still circumstantial. On one hand I'm thinking you could pay her a little visit and ask her a few questions, but if we're wrong, we could ruffle a lot of feathers in Serenity Peak," Gideon said. "It could be problematic. Keep pushing for more evidence and then we can call her in."

"You're right about that," he muttered, knowing that he was being led only by a gut feeling and a missing button on a cloak. "I don't want to do anything to jeopardize the integrity of this office so it might be wise to question several of the choir members to see what it yields. We could also do a handwriting comparison if we feel that Gracelyn is our person of interest."

"I appreciate all of your hard work on this case, Ryan." Gideon pulled out an envelope from his desk and handed it to him. "This was shoved under the door when I came in this morning. It's the same handwriting from the other letter." He stood up from his desk. "I've got to head over to Seldovia to interview a witness for another case I'm working on, but we can discuss whatever's in this note when I get back."

After Gideon departed, Ryan stared blankly at the note, scratching his jaw as confusion swirled over him. What in the world was going on? A second letter? He ripped it open with his finger and pulled the letter out, quickly skimming it.

Dear Ryan,
It's me again. Lula's mother. I've shed a lot of tears over the past few weeks. Something tells me I'm never going to stop crying over my baby. So I've made a decision. I want Lula back. I want to be her mother. And I need your help.

Lula's Mom

Ryan was blown away by the note. Lula's mother wanted to come forward. This investigation might wrap quicker than he'd thought. Lula's mother was having second thoughts about relinquishing her child, just as Skye and Lula were bonding at a fast pace. He had seen cases like this before and he knew the courts liked to reunite babies with their birth parents. If this woman truly wanted Lula back, Ryan knew the law would be on her side. *It's a good thing. Lula should know her birth mother. It's only right. She's realized that she made a mistake in giving her up. Shouldn't she have a chance to make things right?*

What about Skye? The question popped into his mind. Even though her role as a foster mom was always supposed to be temporary, he knew that this would be a crushing blow to her. For a multitude of reasons, Ryan felt protective of Skye. She had been so wounded in the past by her mother's untimely death and Tyler's desertion. He didn't want her to suffer any more hurts. If he could, Ryan would shield her from all the bad things life could throw at a person.

He didn't even want to examine the reasons behind his desire to protect Skye. Maybe it was tied up in his being a state trooper. Or maybe it was something deeper he couldn't afford to admit, not even to himself.

All he wanted to do right now was see her. Perhaps he could do something nice for her and Lula. Ryan missed seeing both of them. It was amazing how much he cared about them. He knew they filled up a void in his life. Every moment he spent in their presence was cherished. Hours after a visit he would still be thinking about them.

A part of him acknowledged that he might be getting too attached. He and Skye were in the friend zone and Lula might be going back to her birth mother. If he continued along this path, it would lead him straight to heartbreak.

"Molly! What a sweet surprise!" Skye said as she ushered her friend inside from the cold. Having her best friend show up at the house was a nice treat on a humdrum day. Sometimes it got a little lonely when Lula went down for a nap and she was alone with nothing but her thoughts to keep her company. Spending so much time at home brought memories of her mother to mind, reminding her that missing her would never go away. Grief was a lifelong journey.

"Well, I know you've been busy with Lula and I've missed seeing your beautiful face, so I decided to come by with lunch." Molly held up a decorative picnic basket.

Skye clapped her hands together with delight.

"Girls' lunch. I love it. Who's minding the store for you?"

"Well, Humbled is doing so well that I've been able to hire on a few new staff members to work part-time hours," Molly said with a huge grin.

Skye was overjoyed for her friend. Getting her business up and running had been no easy feat. Humbled had quickly becoming a favorite coffee establishment in Serenity Peak. Adding on a bookstore had been genius. Molly had worked so hard for her success.

"That's great news," Skye said. "Kira is still helping me out at Sugar's Place, which is truly a blessing. That way I can spend quality time with Lula."

They quickly set up the table for their lunch, wanting to take advantage of Lula's nap time. As they ate salmon and cucumber sandwiches, rosemary chips and a wild berry salad, followed by double chip brownies, the two friends chatted and giggled through the meal.

"I can't believe we didn't hang out at the northern lights viewing," Molly said, regret laced in her words. "What a night that was!"

Skye felt a little guilty that she hadn't sought Molly out. "I ended up watching with Ryan," she admitted. She wanted to confide in her girlfriend about her budding feelings for the handsome lawman.

Molly cocked her head to the side. "Oh, did you? Spill it. I can tell by the look on your face that something happened between the two of you." She leaned across the table. "Am I right?"

Skye's cheeks warmed. "You know me too well." She paused before saying, "We kissed."

Molly let out a gasp. "Seriously?" She rubbed her hands together. "I should have known you couldn't stay indifferent to him for long. Not with that gorgeous face of his."

"He is pretty easy on the eyes," Skye agreed, letting out a groan.

"What's the matter? Was it disappointing?" Molly asked, leaning farther across the table with an expectant look on her face.

Skye burst out laughing. "It was absolutely the best kiss of my life."

Molly's eyes bulged. "So, what's the problem?"

"It can't go anywhere between us. He's a really good guy but—"

"But you're not ready to get involved with anyone?"

"Yes, that's exactly it, and there's already been a little gossip about us, which is the last thing I need or want." Skye threw her hands up in the air. "The reality is that I'm not sure I'm ready for a relationship, Molly. The thought of being hurt again really scares me." She sighed. "I don't want to go through that ever again."

"But if you really like him…" Molly trailed off.

"I do," Skye acknowledged, "but I've got to keep my attention focused on Lula and getting my certification."

Her friend nodded. "Lula's really blessed to have you in her life. You're such a devoted foster mother. I think you've found your calling. Motherhood suits you."

Molly's encouraging words were wonderful to hear. She didn't want to let Lula go. Not ever. Maybe there was a way to keep Lula in her life forever…? She needed to work harder than ever to obtain her certification because that would bring her one step closer to achieving her heartfelt goal. She was attending all her training sessions and fulfilling all the requirements such as the home visitation, background check, references and fingerprinting, but the entire process took time. She would have to exercise patience and not expect immediate gratification.

The passage from Psalms 37:4 came to mind. *Delight thyself also in the LORD: and He shall give thee the desires of thine heart.*

This was what she truly wanted for her future. Motherhood. Lula. Creating a safe space for her foster child and filling her life with joy. For now, she was going to keep her eye on gaining her certification and making her foster mother status official. This wasn't simply about Lula. There could be other children in need of a home in the months and years ahead. She had her hands full as it was with these specific goals. A romance with Ryan could only serve to complicate her life and distract her from her agenda.

A few days after the northern lights watch, Ryan drove over to Sugar Works, intent on checking in on Skye and Lula. The back roads were slippery from sleet and ice, so he paid extra attention to make sure his vehicle didn't slide off the road. When he was a few feet away from the house, he spotted a familiar-looking figure standing beside a green truck in the driveway.

Skye had her hands on her hips, and he watched as she kicked the front tire with her booted foot. Hmm. Something was up with her truck. And it was an issue that greatly annoyed Skye.

Ryan guided his vehicle over toward Skye's truck just as she spotted him driving up. Once he got out of his cruiser he walked toward her, quickly swallowing up the space between them.

"I've never been so happy to see anyone in my entire life," she said, sounding out of breath. Her cheeks were flushed from the cold and her hair was windswept.

"What happened?" he asked. He didn't see any signs of an accident, which was good.

"I was about to drive Lula over to Poppy's clinic for a doctor's appointment and my truck wouldn't start. I have no idea what the problem is other than the battery sometimes reacts to cold temperatures by freezing up," she said. "I have jumper cables in the back of my truck."

"You know how to jump-start a vehicle?" he asked. He knew he sounded dumbfounded but he had always viewed her as a daddy's girl, one who wouldn't get her hands dirty.

She gaped at him. "Of course I do. My dad taught me when I was fourteen years old. Why is that surprising?" she asked, tapping her foot while her arms were folded across her chest.

"No, I was just…caught off guard," he admitted. "No offense, but I've always thought of you as someone who wouldn't…" He fumbled for the right words, ones that wouldn't insult her.

"I guess there's more to me than meets the eye," Skye said. "Can we get this started? We've only been outside for a few minutes and the car is still warm but I'm a little worried about Lula sitting in a cold car."

"You said that the two of you were headed to the clinic? What's going on with Lula?" he asked, moving toward the truck.

She bit her lip. "Lula's breathing is a bit labored and I'm afraid she's coming down with something. I really don't want to miss this appointment."

"Skye, in order to save time, why don't I take you to the clinic? We can jump-start your truck later on," Ryan suggested. He knew Skye wouldn't forgive herself if she missed the doctor's appointment. "Will that work for you?"

A look of relief swept over Skye's face. "Oh, Ryan. That would be wonderful. Let me grab Lula."

"Allow me," Ryan said, stepping in front of her and pulling the truck's back door open. The moment he laid eyes on the little girl, something in his chest tightened. She was fast asleep with her thumb lodged in her little mouth. Long dark lashes gave her a delicate air. He lifted her gently out of the vehicle and walked with her back toward his own car. "Why don't you hop in. I can take care of this," he assured Skye, who was watching him like a hawk. He almost wanted to chuckle at her protective Mama Bear stance.

It took no time at all for him to take the car seat out of Skye's truck and safely secure Lula in the back seat. He pivoted and got behind the wheel, then rapidly made his way off the property toward Poppy's clinic. He sensed Skye's nervousness and her desire to get answers as soon as possible. He flew past the beautiful Alaskan scenery, making sure to stay reasonably within the speed limit. Fifteen long minutes later they arrived at their destination.

Skye turned toward him and placed her hand on his arm. An immediate awareness of her touch caused his skin to tingle. "We got here with a few minutes to spare, thanks to you. I'm super grateful."

"No need to thank me," Ryan said. "It's all in the job description," he said with a smile.

She smiled back before unbuckling her belt.

"Well, let's get Lula inside and get her situated," Ryan said, feeling a bit of urgency himself. Lula was so little and vulnerable. Skye wasn't the only one who cared about her welfare. He was also invested in the well-being of the little charmer.

Once they stepped inside the clinic it wasn't long before Skye and the baby were whisked into a private room. Ryan didn't plan to follow, until Skye turned back toward him and beckoned him into the room. "Join us, please," she said. "I'd like another pair of ears."

"Of course," Ryan said, stepping into the small room and closing the door behind him.

By this point Lula was wide-awake and he could see her chest rising up and down at a rapid pace. He didn't want to alarm Skye, but he also heard a little whistling sound emanating from her.

Lord, please watch over this precious baby. She's already been through so much in her young life. Please grant her complete healing.

"Well, hello there," Poppy exclaimed as she entered the room after a few knocks. "What brings you in today?"

"I'm a little worried about Lula's ragged breathing. She's been sniffly and now this. I wanted you to check her out before it gets any worse," Skye explained.

Poppy looked over at Ryan. "Are you here for moral support?"

"Absolutely," Ryan said. "This little lady has a huge fan club."

"I can understand why," Poppy said as she began her examination. She proceeded to check the infant's ears, take her temperature and listen to her heart and lungs.

"Hmm. Her breathing is a little choppy, which could be any number of things," Dr. Matthews said. "She could have gotten a little virus that brought out a tendency toward asthma. Or it could just be a respiratory infection that's affecting her lungs. Unfortunately, we don't have any family history, so we really don't know if there's any asthma in her genetics."

"So you think she might have asthma?" Skye asked, holding Lula even tighter against her chest.

"It's a possibility, but we rarely diagnose children at her age. It could simply be her body responding to a bad virus. We have a lot of them circulating in the community." Poppy shook her head. "I've had dozens of kids in my office in the last week or so battling viruses."

"How will you treat this?" Ryan asked. He wanted to fill in the gaps for Skye in case she was too overwhelmed to ask.

"I would like to start her on a nebulizer treatment with the hopes of clearing this up fast. I'll show you how to administer it and send you home with a nebulizer and some medication." She reached out and put her arm around Skye. "Don't worry, Mama. She's going to be just fine."

He could tell Skye was trying her best to be stoic, but by the little creases on her forehead, he knew she was worried.

"And I'm going to pay close attention to the nebulizer instructions," Ryan announced. "So I can step in and help you out at any time. You've got backup."

"I appreciate that, Ryan, more than you'll ever know," Skye said in a low voice.

Poppy cleared her throat. "Okay, then, let's get started. The instructions are pretty easy and I'll start by giving her the first treatment right now."

By the time the appointment was over, Skye

was in a more relaxed mood and she appeared confident about Lula's action plan. After Ryan drove them back to Sugar Works, Skye sat behind the wheel of her car while Ryan gave it a jump start. Lula was sleeping peacefully in the warmth of Ryan's vehicle.

Skye let out a triumphant cry when the truck's engine began to rev. She revved it a few more times before hopping down from the cab. Skye held up her hand for a high five from Ryan, who happily obliged.

"I'm going to let the truck run for a while if that's okay," she said. "Just to make sure."

"Fine by me. You'll just have to put up with my company a little longer," Ryan said in a teasing tone.

"Are you kidding me? You've been our hero today. Honestly, you showed up just in the nick of time. I owe you a debt of thanks."

"In case you haven't figured it out, I like hanging out with you and Lula."

Something hummed and pulsed in the air between them that Ryan couldn't ignore. Try as he might to act as if they were simply in the friend zone, no friend he'd ever had made him feel like this. Skye made him believe he could leap buildings in a single bound.

"We're blessed to have you in our corner." Skye leaned against Ryan's chest and wrapped her arms around him, giving him a huge hug. Ryan placed his arms on her back, not wanting to let go. A light floral scent from her hair filled his nostrils. Skye fit so perfectly in the crook of his arm, almost as if she was meant to be there.

She let go of him just as he was getting used to her nearness. Their gazes locked and he sensed she wanted to share something with him. He wanted to be the person she confided in. A soft place to fall.

"What is it?" he asked. "Are you still worried about Lula?"

"No, I trust Poppy's judgment about her." She fiddled with her fingers. "It's something else. I didn't tell you this the other night, but I've been yearning to share it with someone."

"I'm honored," Ryan said as a warm sensation spread through him.

"You've proven yourself to be a good friend. Trustworthy and loyal," Skye said. "I'm so sorry I lost sight of that when the wedding was called off. I was so wrong."

Trustworthy and loyal.... Guilt seized him by the throat. He hadn't told Skye about the letters he'd received from Lula's mother or about her intention to reclaim her daughter. It made him feel dishonest, especially after she had trusted him to be present at Lula's doctor's appointment.

"I appreciate you're saying that," Ryan said,

somehow managing to speak past the raw sandpaper feeling in his throat.

"I want to share something with you, but we should get Lula inside first," Skye said. His interest piqued, he helped Skye get the baby settled in her crib for a nap, then sat down with her at the kitchen table.

Excitement shimmered in the depths of her eyes. She was beaming. "I'm bursting to tell someone. Oh, Ryan. So far, I'm well on my way toward getting my certification. I couldn't be more thrilled. I know it's going to take some time to complete it, but I'm looking toward the future," she said. "That means I'll be eligible to begin the process for adopting Lula. God has been leading me in this direction for weeks now and I keep trying to push the thought away, but I can't." She pressed her hands to her cheeks. "What do you think? Should I try to make it official?"

Skye shifted around in her chair, unable to sit still. She had put herself out there by telling Ryan about her future plans to adopt Lula and now she was wondering if it had been a mistake. So far he was the only person she had confided in. She hadn't even told Violet or Molly or her father. But now, she couldn't gauge Ryan's reaction. He was simply gaping at her. Did her idea seem too aspirational? Was she being un-realistic?

"So, don't leave me hanging," Skye said. "What do you think? I know it's a long process and it could take a substantial amount of time. Your opinion means a lot to me. After all, you've been part of our story since the beginning." Skye glanced at the baby monitor between them as hot cocoa simmered on the stove.

"Cat got your tongue?" she asked in a teasing tone when he still didn't answer her. Maybe she shouldn't have put him on the spot.

Finally, he spoke. "Skye, I can't think of an-other person in this big wide world who would make a better mother than you." The look ema-nating from his eyes was so deep and powerful. He radiated sincerity.

She felt a huge grin stretching across her face. "I might use you for a character reference if need be." Although she was joking, it wasn't a half bad idea.

Ryan held his hand up as if he were writing with an imaginary pen. "To whom it may con-cern, it doesn't get any better than Skye Drum-mond when it comes to motherhood. She's loving and nurturing and provides a wonderful home life for Lula. A child couldn't ask for a better mother, one who will fill her world with won-der and light."

Tears sprung to Skye's eyes as Ryan recited his fictitious letter. It was heartwarming to know that he thought so well of her as a potential mother for Lula. His willingness to vouch for her could make all the difference in her petition to become an adoptive mother. After all, he was a state trooper and he'd been on the case since the beginning. His standing in the community gave him clout.

"I—I don't know what to say, other than thank you. I'm grateful," she said, reaching out and clasping his hand in hers. He leaned toward her and she quickly closed the distance between them, brushing her lips over his. Even though she knew there were things standing in their way, nothing seemed as important as this moment. The present was so much more powerful than the past. She felt Ryan's fingers brushing her hair away from her face, before they swept across her cheek. This kiss, she thought, was just as wonderful as the first time. An electric current pulsed between them, igniting emotions within her. It felt clear to her that they were no longer just friends. Friends didn't share kisses like this.

"Skye." Ryan murmured her name before he pressed his mouth to hers again. She kissed him back in equal measure, wishing that this moment could last forever. This man brought out feelings she had only dreamt about before now. Everything was sharper. More intense. This kiss was fireworks in February.

When it ended, Ryan leaned his forehead on hers. For a moment it seemed as if nothing really mattered but the here and now.

"Skye, I truly believe you would be a great mother for Lula, but you might want to slow things down a bit. We're in the middle of an investigation into Lula's birth parents and we have some new leads."

Her heart skittered at the realization that there were developments in Lula's case. Skye had no idea where things would end up and it was nerve-racking.

She leaned back, crossed her arms in front of her. "I've been praying for answers… I'm hoping we get resolution, especially for Lula's sake."

"I should get back to work before Gideon sends out reinforcements," Ryan murmured.

"Let me walk you to the door," Skye said, reaching out and taking Ryan's hand. His hand fit perfectly in hers and a part of her didn't want to let go. She was enjoying his company more than she wanted to admit. Getting close to someone was always a risk, especially with her history.

He leaned down and brushed a kiss across her

forehead. "Get some rest while Lula's sleeping. I know you've been run ragged lately."

It felt nice to know Ryan truly cared about her well-being. He was solid in every way imaginable.

"Will I see you at the choir concert next week?" Skye asked. "Lula should be back to normal by then, according to Poppy."

A frown appeared on Ryan's face. "You want to attend the concert?"

"Yes," she said, grinning. "I'm determined to turn over a new leaf and show up for town events. There's nothing better than supporting Serenity Peak's female choir."

He nodded. "You've got that right. Autumn invited me to come, so I'll probably go to support her," Ryan said. "I'll be in touch." With a wave of his hand, he was out the door.

Skye watched as Ryan drove away from the house. She was slightly disappointed that he hadn't suggested they attend the concert together. Unless she was imagining things, he had acted a bit funny when she'd brought up attending the concert. Despite the kisses they had shared, Skye didn't have a single clue how Ryan felt about her.

All the emotions she had been harboring for Ryan rose to the surface in a single instant. She was falling for the handsome state trooper. This man she'd known since they were children had proven himself to be someone she could lean on. He was kind and loyal, with an inner strength and integrity that defined his character. The butterflies in her stomach every time he was in the vicinity served as a telltale sign that he was more than a friend. The tender kisses they had shared gave her hope that he reciprocated her feelings, even though they remained unspoken.

After the humiliation of her canceled wedding, Skye had vowed to closely guard her heart. She'd never imagined that she would fall for someone who had been right under her nose her entire life. But with each passing day her heart was opening up to Ryan like a blossoming flower in springtime.

Despite her best intentions to keep Ryan at a safe distance, her heart was overruling her head. And there didn't seem to be a single thing she could do to stop it.

The entire way back to town, Ryan thought about what Skye had told him about adopting Lula. On one hand the news had completely shocked him, while another part of him knew instinctively that it was exactly right. Skye had been wearing her heart on her sleeve ever since discovering Lula on the porch of Sugar's Place. She was following the yearnings of her heart and he couldn't fault her for that. Clearly, Lula brought joy to Skye's life and she was being led by her faith and her heart to adopt the baby.

He felt incredibly guilty. Ryan was sitting on explosive information about Lula's birth mother and her desire to reclaim her daughter. He'd meant every word he had uttered to Skye about her being a wonderful mother, but a huge lump had been sitting in his throat the entire time. She might never get the opportunity. What if Skye made plans to adopt and then Lula's birth mother blindsided her by taking her baby back? How could he justify keeping silent? It seemed as if Skye might be on a collision course with disaster.

Ryan had almost told Skye everything back at the house, but his duty as a state trooper prevented him from doing so. And if he'd violated his oath by telling her about the contents of the last note, it might have sent Skye into a frenzy, which wouldn't have solved anything. At least he had let her know that he was still investigating the case and getting leads. He had no idea where this was headed. Was Lula's mother serious about getting Lula back? If so, she would have to prove she could provide a stable home for her child. There had been several cases in Alaska where birth parents had successfully lobbied for their parental rights, so it was very possible she would prevail.

And to further complicate matters, Skye wanted to attend the choir concert. It was a perfectly normal thing, he realized. After all, she and Violet had once been members. Skye wasn't focused on the button he'd discovered and the possible link to Lula's mother. Until his earlier update, Skye had probably figured he'd hit a dead end in his investigation. It felt strange that Skye might be in the church watching Lula's birth mother perform without knowing. What if she decided to seize the moment and approach Skye at the event?

There was really nothing to do but allow the situation to unfold. He couldn't stop Lula's mother from coming forward and he couldn't warn Skye that her life was about to be torn apart. Helpless. That was what he was feeling.

Part of turning his life around had been making God his foundation. In moments such as this one, he knew whom to turn to for guidance and comfort. Although he never assumed all of his prayers would be answered, Ryan knew with a deep certainty that God was listening.

He closed his eyes and prayed. *Lord, I sense that You are using me as a channel between Skye and Lula's mother. I want to protect both of them, while making sure Lula's best interests*

*are served. Guide me into being the light in the
darkness.*

Although he was still consumed with worry,
Ryan knew his soul felt lighter after sharing his
fears with God. He wasn't alone in this. Not by
a long shot.

Chapter Eleven

"It's so nice to have you here." Abel squeezed Skye's hand and smiled down at her as they sat side by side at the choir concert. "I've missed attending events with both of my daughters with me. I can't tell you how happy I am that you're by my side tonight." Seeing her father's huge smile made Skye feel as if she'd hung the moon.

"It's nice to be here," Skye said, placing her head on his shoulder. This evening was shaping up to be something wonderful. She could feel it humming in the very air around her.

Her father winked at her. "You have a lovely voice, Skye. Maybe this time next year you could rejoin the choir and sing with these wonderful ladies."

"Who knows? Maybe," she answered, even though she wasn't certain if she would have the time. After all, if her plan came to fruition, she would still have her hands full with Lula and her work at Sugar's Place. She didn't want to be overly optimistic, but she had done a little research on foster families adopting after fostering. It wasn't an uncommon practice, and in many situations it was encouraged. Just thinking about Lula being her officially adopted daughter caused goose bumps to pop up on her arms.

She needed to discuss her plans with her family since it affected them as well. Skye couldn't imagine that they wouldn't be supportive, even if they were a bit surprised by this big move she was prepared to put into motion. But it was clear to Skye that they adored Lula. Her parents had taught her and Violet the value of family ties. Lula was family in every sense of the word. She had a bond with Skye that was as deep as blood.

The interior of Serenity Church was stunning. As a lover of stained-glass windows, Skye always enjoyed gazing at the colors and the craftsmanship. As she looked outside she could see snow falling gently from the sky, providing a stunning backdrop to tonight's event.

She had been a member of this church since she was a small child. The memories of attending services with her family were indelibly imprinted on her heart. Being back inside this sacred place, surrounded by her community, meant the world to her. Several townsfolk passed by her pew and fawned over Lula. It was heartwarming to feel the love and acceptance from people she had known her whole life. Several friends even volunteered to bring their gently used baby clothes and toys over to her house so Lula could use them.

Violet leaned over and whispered, "Don't look now but Ryan just walked in with Judah and Leif." Her sister flashed her a knowing smile. This time Skye didn't bother telling Violet there wasn't anything brewing between herself and the handsome lawman.

She tried not to turn around, but she couldn't resist glancing over her shoulder. Ryan looked dashing in a dark jacket, tie and a pair of cords. She waved at him and he smiled in her direction. Skye wanted him to come sit beside her so she could enjoy the concert with him, but he took a seat in the front with his family.

Before, she would have worried about being the subject of town talk if she sat with Ryan, but lately she had pushed those fears to the side. She was proud of herself. She was growing as a person by leaps and bounds. Her father had told her a year ago that she was hiding her light under a bushel. At the time she hadn't wanted to listen or absorb his message about shrinking herself down out of a sense of shame, but now she fully understood. And it was something she hoped to teach Lula as the girl grew up and became a woman. Being true to oneself was the highest way to truly love yourself.

As the concert started, Lula began to wiggle around as if she was trying to dance to the music. Abel held her in his arms, looking the part of the proud grandpa. A feeling of contentment swept through Skye. If anyone had told her that she would be this happy right now, she wouldn't have believed it for a second. And it wasn't only because of Lula. Ryan had become a strong force in her life, someone who was nurturing and supportive. All things considered, Skye was on top of the world. Everything in her life was coming together in ways she had never imagined.

In the dark days, weeks and months after being jilted at the altar, Skye had prayed for a moment such as this one. Hope hung in the air around her. There was so much to look forward to and she was filled with anticipation. Finally, she was living again. As the beautiful voices filled the church, a sense of peace settled over her. This performance felt like a symphony for the soul—uplifting and inspiring.

After the concert came to an end, Skye mingled with the townsfolk at a reception in the church basement. Her heart beat a fast rhythm when Ryan sought her out. She couldn't ever remember her hands getting moist or her pulse racing due to a man's proximity. Even her ex-fiancé hadn't elicited this type of response from her.

"I hope you enjoyed the concert as much as I did," Ryan said with a smile. "Those ladies have some powerful voices."

"Very much so," Skye said. "It was nice hearing so many of my favorite worship songs."

"I noticed Lula enjoyed it as well," Ryan said, grinning as he looked over at her. Once again the infant was the center of attention as Abel showed her off to his friends. Everyone was oohing and aahing over her. She was grateful Lula was being admired and not whispered about.

"She's very musical," Skye gushed. "I need to find some ways to stimulate that interest. Maybe when she gets a little older I can sign her up for music enrichment classes." Already her mind was racing with ideas. She didn't want to limit Lula in any way. The possibilities were endless.

A strange expression crossed over Ryan's face. "Skye, maybe you shouldn't plan too much in advance, just in case."

"What do you mean?" she asked, knitting her brows together.

"I told you that Lula's case is still under investigation with leads coming in. What if you don't end up adopting Lula?" Ryan asked, his expression shuttered.

Hurt rippled through her. "I'm a bit confused.

I thought you were on board with my plan to adopt Lula down the road. All of a sudden you're expressing concerns. What's changed?"

"Nothing's changed. I believe in you, Skye. I want all of your dreams to come true. Trust me, I do." He reached out and swept his knuckles across her cheek. "I just don't want you to get hurt if this doesn't go your way."

He was talking in circles, almost as if he knew something she didn't. "Why wouldn't it? I'm simply trying to be hopeful. I'm getting my certification and I've been the one taking care of Lula ever since she was left at Sugar's Place." She stood straighter. It was hard not to feel defensive at a moment like this. Didn't he think she was good enough?

Ryan held up his hands. "Please. I'm not asking you to justify anything. You're more than qualified to be an adoptive mother."

She ran a shaky hand through her hair. "I'm happier than I've been in years. Do you understand what that feels like for me? I'm not hiding away or beating myself up for something I didn't have any control over." She paused to take a breath. "I really want to believe that wonderful things are right around the corner. And part of that is tied in to making things official with Lula becoming my adopted daughter. I'm not expecting it to happen right away. I know this could take a long time. Is there a chance I might get hurt or disappointed? Of course there is, but I'm choosing to take a leap of faith and trust myself and the process."

Don't cry. Don't cry, she urged herself. *Stay strong.*

"And I had hoped you would believe in me too," Skye said, her voice cracking as she turned and walked away.

Ryan let out a groan. He'd fumbled pretty badly with Skye. His intentions had been good, but his delivery had gone sideways. He hadn't meant for his words to distress her, but he'd known right away by her shattered expression that he had.

How did one shield someone they deeply cared about from potential hurts? Had he done enough to plant a shadow of an idea in Skye's head that adopting Lula might not be as easy as she seemed to think? Should he be doing more to protect her?

The very idea of Skye's hopes and dreams going up in flames made him ache for her. If he could stop all the bad things in life from happening to her, Ryan would do so in an instant. Out of nowhere he realized that he was falling in love with her. He would do anything for this amazing woman. He turned toward the exit, hoping he could find Skye before she left with her family. So much remained unspoken between them and he didn't want her to go to bed tonight thinking he didn't believe in her dreams.

As far as he was concerned, Skye Drummond was capable of achieving anything she set out to do.

"Ryan. I was hoping to see you here tonight." Suddenly, Gracelyn appeared, stepping in front of him.

"Gracelyn," Ryan acknowledged with a nod. All evening he had been trying to figure out the best way to approach her without making a commotion. In his gut he sensed that she was linked with Lula and was possibly her mother. Was that why she was seeking him out right now? Was she going to make a confession and admit to sending him the notes?

"I need to talk to you…" She lowered her voice. "…About Lula." She shifted from one foot to the other. "Privately," she added in a hushed tone, her gaze darting all over the room. There were a handful of people chatting nearby. "Is it okay if we talk in the choir rehearsal room down the hall?"

Ryan nodded. "Sounds good." If this conversation was headed where he thought it might be, a private room was best for all concerned. He walked behind Gracelyn, trying to remind himself to be compassionate and calm. Despite the way this situation would impact Skye, it would surely be a blessing for Gracelyn and her family to have Lula back in their lives.

Once he entered the room behind Gracelyn, a figure stepped out from the shadows. She looked young, no more than seventeen or eighteen, with long dark hair and brilliant blue eyes. Although she looked slightly familiar, Ryan wasn't sure he knew who she was.

"This is my younger sister, Betty," Gracelyn said, glancing at the young woman.

"Hey there," Ryan said. "Nice to meet you." He was a bit confused by her sudden appearance in the midst of a private discussion. He vaguely remembered Gracelyn having a younger sister who was in high school. Maybe she was here for moral support. This situation had to be extremely difficult for the entire family.

Betty shyly extended her hand and he shook it. "It's nice to meet you in person, Ryan," Betty said. I'm the one who's been writing to you. I'm Lula's mother."

Ryan inhaled a ragged breath upon hearing Betty's confession. Gracelyn went to stand by Betty's side and the two sisters tightly held hands. Betty was such a tender age and it broke his heart a little that she had been through so much. Someone her age shouldn't have to navigate such major life issues.

He ran a shaky hand across his face. "I have to admit that I didn't see this coming," he said. "Gracelyn, I thought you were the one writing to me."

Gracelyn shook her head. "No, although I did encourage my sister to reach out to you once we heard you were looking for Lula's birth mother."

"I was searching," Ryan said, "but there wasn't much leading me in Betty's direction. I found a button from a choir cloak outside Sugar's Place, which led me to the woman's choir. When I attended a rehearsal I noticed yours was missing from your cloak. And from what I witnessed that night there seemed to be some tension."

Gracelyn shrugged. "I missed a bunch of rehearsals after Lula was born. Some of the women didn't think it fair that I had two solos after skipping practice. None of them know that Betty is Lula's mother."

"I wore Gracelyn's cloak the morning I left Lula at Sugar's Place," Betty admitted. "It was nice and warm on a chilly morning. I kept Lula underneath the fabric until I saw Skye coming along the path." Her eyes began to tear up. "I never put her in harm's way."

"She even stayed until she saw Skye discover

Lula," Gracelyn added, placing a protective arm around her sister. "She loves her daughter."

"Everyone, including Doc Poppy, knew that you kept Lula safe at all times. Please know that, Betty," Ryan said. She was so young to have made such a huge life decision. He hated thinking she might be beating herself up for leaving her baby at Sugar's Place.

"I do love Lula, and although it may seem selfish of me, I want her back." Tears streamed down Betty's face. "I didn't think that I could raise her without her father in the picture."

"Where is he, Betty?" Ryan asked. Was he still in Serenity Peak?

Betty looked at him with a forlorn expression. "Ever since I told him that I was having our baby he's distanced himself from me…and Lula. He doesn't want to be a father. And he never wanted me to raise our child."

"That was the main reason she left Lula," Gracelyn explained. "She didn't think she could raise her daughter by herself at seventeen years old. She agonized over the decision, but she's still in high school with no way of supporting herself, never mind a child. I wish that I could have stepped in to raise the baby but I have some health issues that complicate matters."

It was all making sense. The Handel parents had both passed away a few years ago and

Gracelyn and her brother, Josh, had been taking care of Betty. How could a child give birth to a baby and feel confident about raising her?

"And Sugar's Place? Why did you pick that location?" he pressed. He didn't want to overwhelm Betty with questions, but he needed answers, not only in his official capacity, but for Skye. Perhaps down the road it would make her feel better to know certain facts.

"Skye has always been such a lovely person. I knew she would take care of my baby as if she was her very own. Not to mention that I'd heard the Drummonds were a foster family," Betty said, the corners of her mouth curving in the hint of a smile. "I think it was a great decision of mine to choose someone who would love my baby."

"And she has," Ryan said. "Fully. Wholly. Without a single reservation… She couldn't love Lula any more than she does. It's just not possible."

"That's such a blessing and I'm so grateful to her for everything she's done," Betty said, wiping away tears. "I know she's been through a lot, so I hope Lula made her smile again."

Ryan felt tears pricking at his own eyes. This was an emotional moment, and it didn't escape him that Skye should be here. She was the one who had taken care of Lula day in and day out, asking for nothing in return. She should be standing here accepting thanks from Betty and telling her about her daughter's milestones. She'd earned the right to be here at this meeting with Lula's mother.

"So, you're coming forward to get Lula back?" Ryan asked. He held his breath waiting for her answer. Maybe she wasn't going to reclaim her daughter, he told himself. Perhaps this would all work out in the end. *Lord, please make a way.*

Betty glanced over at Gracelyn, who nodded. "Yes, I want to be with my daughter," the teen said in a trembling voice. "Coming clean with you is the first step."

"We did some research," Gracelyn said, her voice ringing out with authority. "In most cases, the rights of birth mothers are upheld."

Ryan didn't disagree, but a numb feeling was creeping across his body. All he could think about was Skye and the devastation this would bring to her world.

Skye will be hurt. Skye will be blindsided. Skye won't know what hit her. The agonizing thoughts rolled around in his head until he thought he might explode.

"Before this goes any further, I'd like to be the one to tell Skye and tell her about you," he said. "Lula is part of her world now, so this is going to be a big adjustment."

"That works for me," Betty said in an eager voice. Ryan counted to ten in his head and reminded himself that she was a young girl trying to navigate a stressful situation. She had no idea that Skye would be heartbroken. After all, giving up Lula had been devastating for Betty.

"We'll be in touch," Gracelyn said. "We won't say anything to Child Services until you've spoken to Skye." The sisters walked out of the room hand in hand, leaving Ryan feeling more troubled and anxious than he could ever remember.

Although he had volunteered himself to be the bearer of bad news, his nerves were frazzled. How in the world was he going to break the heart of the woman he was falling in love with?

Chapter Twelve

The morning after the choir concert, Skye was baking sourdough cornbread and blueberry scones. They would go nicely with the berry jam she had canned months ago. She was hoping to bring a basket over to Ryan's place later this afternoon as an apology of sorts. It was his day off and she could text him later to make sure he was at home for her delivery.

She had been defensive last night when Ryan had challenged her a little bit about adopting Lula. In hindsight, Skye wished she had remained cooler under pressure. Ryan was in her corner, and she knew he had meant well. Her nervousness over the possibility of not being able to adopt Lula had impacted her reaction last night. She had reacted with emotion rather than reason.

That was the old Skye. She had grown so much in the last few months. She was proud of the woman she was today and there was no room for backward steps. If she was going to officially become Lula's mother, Skye needed to keep making forward progress. Lula was inspiring her to be a stronger woman.

To allow her time to bake, Violet had brought Lula into town along with her and Chase. They were running errands at the market and picking up a few clothing items for both Chase and Lula. Skye appreciated having alone time while she was baking.

A loud knocking emanated from the front door. She let out a frustrated noise—she was up to her elbows in flour and sugar. Skye quickly took a batch of scones out of the oven, then wiped her hands on her apron. She walked to the front door and pulled it open. A huge grin tugged at her lips when she saw Ryan standing on her doorstep.

"Hey there, Ryan. What brings you over here so bright and early?' Skye waved him into the house. "Shouldn't you be sleeping in on your day off?" she asked in a playful tone. He was such a hardworking member of law enforcement. He absolutely deserved a break from his official duties.

"I needed to see you," Ryan said in a clipped tone.

Her pulse quickened. Ryan's words were music to her ears. She found herself missing him when he wasn't around. Hopefully, he felt the same way about her. Seeing him at the choir concert had been nice, but Ryan had seemed on edge. His vibe had been off and she hadn't been able to ask him if anything was wrong. Instead she'd gotten annoyed at him and left the reception.

"Violet and Chase took Lula into town so I could do some baking. Would you like a scone? They're fresh from the oven." The scones were a perfect golden brown color.

"They smell really good, but I don't have much of an appetite at the moment." His tone hinted at him being downcast. It wasn't like Ryan not to be upbeat and talkative. Again, she wondered what was going on.

"Skye, there's something I need to tell you."

A feeling of dread enveloped her. Hadn't Tyler said those very words to her right before ditching her at the altar? Was Ryan going to take a step back from what they'd been building? If so, she wouldn't be able to hide her heartache. At this point she was falling in love with him and she didn't want to lose him.

"What is it?" Skye asked, her heart in her throat. So many thoughts were racing through her mind. At the moment she just wanted him to rip off the Band-Aid and give it to her straight. If he was going to walk away from her, she wanted to know as soon as possible.

"I've met Lula's mother," Ryan blurted out.

"What?" she asked. She hadn't been expecting that. In an instant, a multitude of questions were on the tip of her tongue.

He nodded. "She's seventeen years old and a high school student."

She raised a hand to her throat. "Who? Who is she?" Skye asked. This moment felt surreal. She was finally going to get answers, yet her stomach was in knots. In a small town like Serenity Peak, she was bound to know the young woman.

"Her name is Betty Handel. Gracelyn's little sister."

Gracelyn had been in school with them, and Skye knew she had been raising Betty for the last few years.

She let out a gasp. "Betty? She's so young," Skye murmured. "She can't be more than nineteen years old, poor thing." She made a tutting sound.

"She's actually only seventeen."

"Oh, yes, you said that… I can totally understand why she didn't feel equipped to raise a baby. She must have been so confused."

"From what she said, Betty didn't think she could raise Lula without the father being present," Ryan explained. "He hasn't been around since she told him that she was expecting a baby."

Her heart was breaking at the idea of Betty being stuck in such an impossible situation. She must have felt so frightened and alone. Skye's stomach clenched just thinking about it. "How awful. I can't imagine going through all of that alone."

"She and Gracelyn seem very close," Ryan said. "She's really been a source of great support for Betty. Gracelyn was helping with the baby before Betty decided to give her up."

Skye swallowed. She began fiddling with her fingers. "Well, did you tell her how well Lula is doing? That she's happy and healthy. And she's loved beyond measure."

He let out a ragged sigh. "Skye, I told her all those things and she's very grateful, but she wants Lula back." He winced. "She's had a change of heart. I know this isn't easy to hear, especially since you want to adopt Lula, but Betty seems like she's prepared to move forward with this."

For a moment it seemed as if time stood still. She heard the words coming out of Ryan's mouth, but she couldn't wrap her head around them. Lula's mother wanted her back? How was that possible after she'd relinquished her? Hadn't she basically demonstrated that she didn't want to be her mother? Skye heard a keening sound that she didn't immediately register as coming from her own body. Her knees buckled and Ryan reached out to catch her.

She was breathing rapidly, and catching her next breath seemed difficult. She was suddenly finding it hard to breathe. Was she having a panic attack? This wouldn't be the first time. She'd had several in the days and weeks after her called-off wedding.

"Hold on. Take a seat while I get you some cold water." Ryan's voice was sure and calm. He gently led her to a chair and sat her down. She put her head in her hands and began to sob softly. Why was this happening? Just when she'd been feeling confident, the rug was being pulled out from underneath her.

"Here you go," Ryan said as he came back into the room and handed her the water.

She took a few sips from the glass, tightly holding it in her grip. Somehow she needed to make sense of this. "How did you find out?" she asked, her voice sounding like a croak.

"Betty and Gracelyn sought me out after the choir concert. We went to a private room where they told me everything."

She knit her brows together. "I don't understand. Why did they come to you?"

He shrugged. "Because I'm law enforcement, I suppose. And Betty knew I was on scene the day you found Lula," he explained. "She also knew that I went to Serenity Church trying to find out about the cloak button I found outside the shop."

Skye's gut clenched tightly. "You never told me that," she said, sputtering.

He sat down next to her. "Skye, I know it might be hard to understand, but information pertaining to cases is confidential. I couldn't tell you."

"Is there anything else that I need to know now?" Skye pressed. She had this sinking feeling in the pit of her stomach that there was more. She hated doubting Ryan and she prayed that she was wrong.

Ryan looked down instead of making eye contact with her. "You should know something else. Betty wrote me letters, only I didn't know it was her at the time. She signed them as Lula's mother."

Skye wrapped her arms around her middle. Ryan had made contact with Lula's mother and hadn't seen fit to tell her? She had been serving the role of foster mom this whole time, yet he hadn't given her an ounce of consideration.

Ryan reached out to touch her and she shrugged him off. "You knew she wanted her back? And you didn't tell me?"

He let out a mournful sound. "I couldn't,

Skye. I wish you would understand that. I was in an impossible situation."

Anger gripped her by the throat. "Sounds more like you *wouldn't* than couldn't." Clearly she meant nothing to him. Less than nothing if he hadn't made any attempts to protect her. She was feeling raw and bruised.

"Please hear me out," he began. "At first Betty was simply expressing regrets in her letter, but then she articulated her desire to reclaim Lula. Before I knew it, Betty and Gracelyn were approaching me at the concert." He threw his hands in the air. "I know you don't want to hear this, but it's always been a possibility that Lula's mother would make a plea to get Lula back. That's what I was trying to tell you last night."

Skye glared at him. "You're right. I don't want to hear that. All I want is for you to tell me that she can't take Lula away from me." She gritted her teeth. "She gave her up. Betty forfeited the right to raise Lula. Didn't she?"

"I wish that I could tell you that, but the law is on Betty's side. She didn't mistreat Lula. Matter of fact, Lula was well cared for and loved. Betty left her at Sugar's Place because she's always admired you and she knew that you would do right by her daughter."

Skye let out a sob. Her entire body was trembling. "So if that's true, then why is she taking her back?"

"Because she regrets giving her away, Skye. And she loves her, probably every bit as much as you do." His tone sounded tender, but it did nothing to pacify her. This wasn't fair. Not to her. Or Lula. The baby would be confused about this back-and-forth. She had settled so nicely into life in the Drummond household.

Something inside her shattered. She was so tired of all of her dreams going up in smoke. Nothing ever worked out for her. She had thought God was answering her prayers with Lula, but it was turning into a nightmare. Her heart was breaking all over again. And it wasn't just the prospect of having Lula ripped away from her. All this time she had been under the belief that Ryan was on her side. She had trusted him.

What a mistake that had been!

"You could have given me a heads-up about this instead of allowing me to be blindsided by the news. At least I could have prepared myself emotionally for this."

Ryan sighed. "I wish that had been possible. Believe me, I do," he said in an anguished tone. "I want to help you through this. Lean on me. I know this is painful and I'll be there to support you."

"No, thank you," she said, bristling. "I think you've already done enough."

Ryan flinched. He paused a moment before saying, "I'm not sure what happens next but I'm going to give you time to absorb this news. Seeing you hurt is the last thing I ever wanted. I need you to know that even though it may not seem that way to you right now."

"Please leave, Ryan. I want to be alone right now." She didn't want to completely break down in front of him. All she wanted to do was curl up into a little ball and cry her eyes out. Instead she walked Ryan to the door, somehow managing to hold her head up high.

As he stood in the doorway, Ryan turned to her again and said, "If you'd like to talk, I'm only a phone call away."

She didn't bother responding to him. Anything she had to say right now would be spoken through a haze of anger. He sent her a mournful look before heading out of the house toward his vehicle.

"I'll never forgive you, Ryan Campbell. Not for as long as I live." Skye uttered the words as she watched him drive away. As bad as the situation was, Ryan had made it even worse by not having her back. The pain enveloping her was twofold. The knowledge that she might soon have to relinquish Lula was heart-wrenching.

But Ryan's withholding crucial information from her felt like a sucker punch in the gut.

What a fool she had been, allowing herself to believe so strongly that things were finally working in her favor. Lula wasn't ever going to be her daughter. Skye wasn't going to be able to adopt her down the road. The painful reality was beginning to settle in. She had endured a broken heart once before and it had brought Skye to her knees, but this was even more agonizing. To lose a child she had begun to think of as her own was unfathomable.

How would she ever be able to say goodbye to Lula?

It was a dreary, overcast day in Serenity Peak with no hint of sunshine. The weather mirrored Ryan's emotions—bleak and downcast. For the first time since he had become a state trooper, he wished he wasn't. He had been placed in no-win situation as far as he was concerned. And he'd definitely lost.

He had driven to the harbor on instinct, seeking a tranquil spot to think about how he should proceed with Skye. Ever since he was small, this area had been a haven for him. If he wasn't on the Fishful Thinking with his uncle and father, he'd been dreaming about the brilliant waters of Kachemak Bay. He had long ago realized that fishing was in his bloodline and would always be a part of him even if he wasn't a fisherman by trade.

He quickly spotted his father and uncle in the distance on the deck of the boat. Ryan waved in their direction and walked over. The two brothers made a great team along with the rest of the crew. Uncle Judah's enterprise was very successful.

"Hey there. How's it going?" Ryan asked as he stepped onboard. He was trying to sound upbeat despite feeling as if he was coming apart at the seams.

"What brings you out to the harbor?" Uncle Judah asked with a grin. "Do you want to help us clean some of our catch?"

"I seem to remember him saying he wasn't ever doing that again," his father said with a chuckle. "That was always his least favorite part of going out on your boat."

Ryan couldn't even summon up any laughter. His heart didn't feel light or playful. Instead he heaved a big sigh. It felt as if a huge weight sat on his shoulders.

"I always come here when I need to think. The water always draws me in. It must be in the blood," he said, smiling tightly.

"Hey, what's bothering you?" his father asked. "That's not the smile of a happy man. I thought everything was going great in your life."

"It's not about me, not really," Ryan said, shoving his hands in his pocket. He didn't want to burden his family with his problems, but as always, his father quickly picked up on his demeanor. Ryan had never been good at masking his emotions.

"Must be work, then," Uncle Judah said. "Problems with a case?"

"I can't reveal too much, but you know the baby that was left at Sugar's Place?" he asked. At this point, the whole town had heard the news.

Leif nodded.

"Well, Skye has fallen head over heels for the girl, so much so that she wants to adopt her."

"Isn't that good news?" Judah asked, his brows knit together. "Skye deserves some happiness after all that drama with Tyler. And babies need forever families."

"They sure do. And Skye does deserve happiness," he said with a nod. "But the birth mother wants Lula back. She's putting in a request later on today to assume custody," he explained. "I had to break the news to Skye. Needless to say, she was devastated by this turn of events."

Judah let out a low whistle. "That's rough."

"You seem to care a lot about Skye, son," Leif said, placing his arm on Ryan's shoulder. "It's pretty obvious."

"I do have feelings for her," he said, trying to

ignore the squeezing sensation in his chest. It hurt to even think about Skye right now since she'd made it clear that she no longer trusted him. All he'd done was to try and perform his official job duties and help Skye out with Lula, only to have it all crash down around him. He and Skye had patched up their previous issues and become close. Romance had been brewing between them. But now he felt foolish to have even harbored such thoughts. Skye had always been unattainable, and it now seemed as if she always would be.

"We've been spending a lot of time together, which has been great. But she's not too happy with me at the moment because I didn't give her a heads-up about Lula's mother wanting her back," Ryan explained. "To her it felt like a betrayal."

"So I assume you knew this information in a law enforcement capacity?" his father asked.

"Yeah, Lula's mother was reaching out to me as a state trooper. I couldn't share it with Skye for that very reason. Despite my feelings for her, I was duty bound to keep quiet because I was investigating the case." He bit down on the inside of his cheek. "This whole thing is awful."

Judah shook his head. "Surely she'll understand that you didn't have a choice. She might just need some time to process everything."

Ryan wasn't so certain. The expression on Skye's face had been a mix of fury and heart-break. His insides were torn up just thinking about the situation. Skye's generosity had led to her heart being shattered again.

"I hope she'll be able to forgive me and I'm praying she'll understand that I was stuck in an impossible situation. I'm not sure she ever thought Lula's birth mother would make an appearance," Ryan said. "She's been so wrapped up in creating this beautiful life for Lula that she allowed herself to ignore that possibility. I wish I didn't feel so guilty."

Uncle Judah nodded. "When we were kids our Pops always quoted Luke 12:2. 'For there is nothing covered that shall not be revealed.'"

"In other words, this was always going to come out one way or the other," his father said, placing his hand on Ryan's shoulder again. "Lula's mother has had a change of heart. You've got nothing to feel guilty about, son."

Two of the people he most admired in the world were serving as great sounding boards and lifting him up. He felt much better now that they had shared their pearls of wisdom. He only wished he could make Skye understand that he had an oath to uphold. No matter how much he cared for her, violating that duty would have been wrong.

"How do you feel about Lula's birth mother?" Judah asked.

He shrugged. "I feel sorry for her. She was in a bad spot and she made a decision she regrets. Lula deserves to know the truth about her birth parents. Everyone should know where they came from. I'm just heartbroken for Skye that she's going to have Lula taken away from her."

"Skye might be disappointed and saddened, but she'll get past it. She's a strong young woman." His father sounded so confident and sure, but he hadn't seen Skye with Lula. He didn't know her heart like Ryan did.

Would she really rebound from this as his father believed? She had already weathered heartbreak over her canceled wedding and the death of her mother. Caring for the baby had given her a purpose. Her heart had healed. She loved Lula in ways she had never imagined possible. Her big goal was to officially adopt her and make Lula her very own. And now, those dreams had been crushed.

Chapter Thirteen

Skye gazed out the window of Sugar's Place, watching as the snow drifted down from the heavens. Despite the turmoil raging in her heart, the landscape was tranquil. Birch trees were covered in a light coating of snow and the sky was a shade of gray that hinted at a coming storm. She would be closing the store early today due to a big snow and ice storm that was coming in later this afternoon. Lula was a few feet away, playing in the portable playpen she'd set up near the register. Skye couldn't stop looking at the baby.

It was as if she was trying to imprint Lula on her mind's eye before Betty took her back. She had also ramped up her photo taking, knowing one day she would be able to look back at the pictures and recall these precious moments. Maybe at that point she would feel joy rather than pain.

The past few days had been heart-wrenching. She had vowed not to cry in front of Lula and, so far, she'd been strong. Until she laid her head down to go to sleep. Tears came in the hours between darkness and dawn when she was alone with her thoughts. She had been trying to soak up all of the moments she possibly could with Lula before Betty formally assumed custody. The situation was nerve-racking. She still had no idea how the process would work. Her nerves were on edge as she waited for an official phone call. Although a part of her wanted to reach out to Betty, she wasn't sure if it was appropriate under the circumstances.

Maybe she could ask Ryan. The thought popped into her head before she could cast it off. She and Ryan weren't speaking at the moment. And she missed him terribly. The sound of his voice. His silly jokes. The way he checked in on her and Lula. The kindness that emanated from deep inside of him. Everything about the tenderhearted lawman was dear to her.

But he had betrayed her trust in him and that was something she couldn't abide. Not after everything she had been through with Tyler. She felt sick to her stomach for even comparing Ryan to her ex-fiancé. Ryan was a wonderful man of faith who was caring and loving. Had she judged him too harshly?

The tinkling sound of the bell above the doorway drew her attention to the entrance. Abel was standing there covered in snowflakes. He began vigorously brushing the snow away from his hat and clothing. Due to his large frame and height he looked like the abominable snowman, which brought a smile to her face.

"Daddy. I wasn't expecting to see you here," Skye said. Since the sap from the birch trees needed to be placed into jars on the production line, her father was pretty busy these days. He was a perfectionist who oversaw every aspect of Sugar Works from tapping the birch trees to inspecting the product.

"I wanted to check in on my girls and make sure you got home safely."

Skye let out a chuckle. "We live just down the road. Plus, I have my truck today." Since Lula was a growing girl, the carrier was getting much heavier to carry on her trek to the shop. Having the truck outside was convenient.

Abel shrugged out of his jacket and took off his boots. "Can I bother you for a hot cocoa? It's pretty raw out there."

"No bother at all. Matter of fact, I'll make two." Seeing her father was a nice pick-me-up on a dreary day. He always made her soul feel lighter.

A few minutes later she returned with a tray carrying two cups of hot chocolate and two vanilla scones. Her father was looking down into the playpen and making goofy faces at the baby, who smiled and gurgled at him in an adoring way.

"I'm back," she announced, placing the tray down on a small coffee table. She couldn't help but grin as Abel took the seat opposite her. He was such a large man that he looked like a giant sitting at the dainty table. She placed his drink in front of him, then blew on her own to cool it down before taking a sip.

"This really hits the spot," he said after raising the mug to his lips and taking a lengthy sip.

"It's my own concoction," she admitted. "I've been thinking we might sell it here at the store, maybe give it a catchy name. Sugar Bombs or Sugar Rush. Something catchy. And I could design some eye-catching packaging."

His eyes widened. "Skye, that's a tremendous idea. I love your entrepreneurial spirit."

She smiled. At least that was something exciting to look forward to. It was so difficult to walk around feeling downcast but having to plaster a smile on your face so others wouldn't worry. Judging by the look on her father's face, she wasn't fooling him any.

Abel drummed his fingers on the side of his mug. "How are you doing with…everything?" She had cried the other night while telling Violet and her father about Betty's plan to claim her parental rights. As always, they had been supportive and comforting. She sensed that her father was being delicate with his words. No doubt he worried that she might start crying all over again. Frankly, she was all cried out.

She shrugged. "I'm doing all right. I'm trying to make the most of the time I have left with Lula. Sadly, she'll never remember this time with me. It will almost be as if it never happened."

"That's not true, sweetheart. Your decision to foster Lula came from an altruistic place. You wanted to step in the breach and help out a child in need. That's the most beautiful act of all." His voice rang out with passion. "And you did help Lula. Whether or not she remembers isn't what matters most. You've come back to life in the last few weeks and it's brought joy to the people who love you."

"She brought out the best in me," Skye admitted. She couldn't help but wonder if all the personal growth she'd been experiencing would now grind to a halt without Lula in her life.

"You've grown up a lot, Skye. And I'm so proud of you for having gone through so much yet you've emerged stronger and more focused. Honestly, you deserve credit for doing all the hard work to push past adversity. Lula inspired you, but you did the heavy lifting."

"I appreciate that," Skye said, her cheeks warming.

"And there's someone else who's been a big part of your journey," he said, narrowing his gaze as he stared into her eyes.

"Who do you mean?" she asked, genuinely confused.

"I believe Ryan had a big part in it." Before she could respond, he held up his hands. "Hear me out. I watched as your whole world crumbled a few years ago. You were at rock bottom. I never thought I would see you smile again the way you were at the northern lights watch with Ryan. Or all the other times he came by the house."

Skye bit her lip. "I never thought I would have feelings for him, especially since he's always been such good friends with Tyler."

Her father waved that off. "Newsflash. Those two haven't been close in years. Ryan is on a different path and he wanted to distance himself from Tyler's chaotic lifestyle."

"Why didn't he tell me all this?" she asked her father. She'd fretted about their friendship, all while falling for Ryan. Although he'd told her that they hadn't seen each other in months, Ryan hadn't told her about the state of their friendship in any great detail.

"Maybe he didn't want to bring up someone

who'd brought you pain." Her father shrugged. "Or maybe he simply didn't think it mattered so much to you. I have no idea. But I do know that he's been such a godsend for you…and Lula."

He was right. Ryan had given himself so freely to her, first through friendship and then something more that she still couldn't define.

"It's just confusing because he hid stuff from me. He didn't have my back," she said feebly.

"Didn't he?" her father asked. "From where I'm standing, he did all the important things other than betray his oath as a state trooper. What kind of a man would he be if he did that?"

Skye fumbled to find something to say, but she was rendered speechless. Abel always had a way of breaking things down into their simplest components. She had been wrong. Ryan hadn't betrayed her. She couldn't place her sorrow on his shoulders. And he had tried to warn her the night of the choir concert, but she hadn't wanted to listen.

She sighed. "I've been so wrong, but I don't know what to say to him…how to make things right," she said, feeling even more lost at the knowledge that she had messed up so badly.

"Ryan makes you happy. That's a precious thing, something to be cherished." Her father placed his hand over hers. "Don't squander this chance at happiness. Don't let pride trip you up," he warned.

"But what if he doesn't want to talk to me?" Fear rose inside of her at the thought of severing ties with Ryan. The truth was she wanted him in her life. The thought of losing him and Lula at the same time was unbearable.

"There's only one way to find out. Step out on a limb of faith, my sweet girl. Be courageous." He picked up his hot cocoa and took a long sip.

As they rode out the storm later that evening, Skye vowed to come up with a way to make things right with the man she loved.

The calm after the snowstorm was something Ryan had always enjoyed. Now that the roads were plowed and he had checked on a few elderly townsfolk to make sure they were okay, he could enjoy the beauty of his surroundings. Mother Nature had showed off and dropped snow all over Serenity Peak. The fluffy white stuff was piled up as far as the eye could see. This type of wintry weather was his favorite, although Alaska was magnificent all year round.

At the moment he was checking out the roof of Serenity Church. He had received a call a short while ago from one of the parishioners that the roof had been impacted by the storm. Since Ryan had some roofing skills he'd headed over to help. Thankfully, the structure wasn't in danger of caving in, although it had sustained minor damage. He felt confident that he could make the roof repairs as soon as the snow melted a little bit. He loved being part of the church community and this was his way of giving back.

The sound of a vehicle door slamming caused him to turn around. He carefully stepped down from the ladder as soon as he spotted Skye standing by her truck. For a moment he wanted to rub his eyes to make sure he wasn't seeing things. Skye was here. She was making her way toward him, although her body language seemed a bit uncertain.

All of a sudden he was tongue-tied at the sight of her. She had been at the center of his thoughts for days. His heart was in his throat and his entire body had tensed up as she approached him. He prayed she hadn't come by to tell him off again. He wasn't sure he could take any more rejection from her. As it was, he was barely holding up. Not hearing from her or being able to swing by the house to see her and Lula was eating him up inside.

"Skye," he said with a nod, barely able to get her name out past the scratchy feeling in his throat.

"Gideon told me that you were out here, so I

took a chance you would still be looking at the roof."

"Yeah, I'm assessing the damage. I suppose it could have been a lot worse."

She visibly took a deep breath. "I owe you the world's biggest apology. I'm ashamed of the way that I acted the other day. None of it is your fault." She was tugging at her mittens, looking ill at ease.

He let a few moments of silence stretch out between them.

"So, is that it?" he asked. "You're not even going to grovel just a little bit?"

Skye's jaw dropped and she looked at him with big eyes. Ryan couldn't keep his composure. He started laughing, his shoulders heaving with the effort. He was so relieved she was speaking to him again. Almost instantly, a huge weight had been lifted off his shoulders.

Skye pressed a hand to her chest. "Oh, phew. You were teasing me. That's a relief."

"Sorry, I couldn't resist," Ryan said. "Honestly, I'm just happy to see you here. I haven't been able to think of much else, other than the way we parted." He reached out and brushed his knuckles across her cheek. "It didn't sit well with me."

"Me neither," she whispered, a sheen of tears glistening in her eyes. "I've had some time to think and pray. It was good to do some self-re-flection. I can't pretend that I'm not upset about the situation, but I'm also grateful."

"Grateful?" Ryan asked. He was taken aback since she was on the precipice of having to say goodbye to Lula.

She nodded. "Yes, I'm thankful for all this time I've had with Lula. I was blessed to be the one to find her. And it seems Betty singled me out for that role, which means a lot to me. I was so fortunate to be Lula's foster mother and I wouldn't trade the experience for anything in the world." She swallowed hard before she continued speaking. "The time I've spent with Lula has shown me that my heart isn't defective. It's strong and powerful. Because of Lula I trust my-self more and I know that I'm worthy of good things."

His gut twisted painfully. "I'm sorry you ever doubted that in the first place. You're a good woman, Skye Drummond. You always have been." Memories of her as a sweet, caring child swept over him. She'd always been the one to befriend the new student or stick up for anyone being bullied. She had always done the right thing regardless of who was watching. And she had grown into a magnificent woman, one who put others first and radiated her own special light for all to see. She was a rare gem.

"And it's not just Lula who's changed my world. It's you as well, Ryan." She was looking him straight in the eye, her gaze unwavering. "I'm grateful for you."

He didn't want to get too excited. Not just yet. Maybe she was referencing their friendship rather than something else.

She reached out for his hand and squeezed it. "You've been so wonderful to me. And that's why I feel so ashamed of the way I lashed out at you. What's that saying about hurting the ones you love?" They locked gazes. "I love you, Ryan. With everything going on with Lula it may seem like the wrong time to say it, but—"

Ryan placed his finger on her lips. "Skye, there will never be a wrong time for you to say those words to me. By the way, I love you too. And if I'm being honest, those feelings have been percolating for quite some time."

Skye's face lit up like pure sunshine. "Oh, Ryan. That makes me so happy. I never thought that I would fall in love again. What I feel for you is stronger than anything I've ever known. It's real and true."

"I know you've been through a lot and there's no way I would ever put you through any heartache. That's a promise." His words were a sacred vow to Skye.

"I do know that. You opened my heart up with

your kindness and the tender way you treated me. That's why I fell in love with you." Every time Skye said those precious words out loud Ryan felt about ten feet tall. His heart was hammering inside his chest and he wondered if she could hear it thumping.

"And if I hadn't found Lula that day we might not have reconnected," Skye said, "so she's brought countless blessings along with her. I can't wallow in sadness anymore. That's why I'm trying to see the glass as half full."

"You're right. Lula led me straight to you," Ryan said. "And I'm not going to let you be sad, not after all you've done for Lula. Lean in to that feeling of gratitude. You'll be better for it."

She nodded. "I'm hoping Betty allows me to be a part of Lula's life, even if it's simply limited contact. Maybe she'll let me visit on her birthday or on special occasions like Christmas." She shook her head, blond curls swirling around her shoulders. "I just can't imagine her not being in my life at all."

He placed an arm around her shoulder and pulled her against his side. "I think she'll be reasonable. She's young and I sense she has a good heart. By the way, she thinks the world of you." He winked at her. "That means she has good taste."

"That's reassuring," Skye said in a soft voice.

"I have no idea where things go from here with Lula, but I know that I can get through it with you by my side."

"Just try and get rid of me," Ryan said, pulling her toward him so that he could place a tender kiss on her lips. "I'm yours for as long as you want me."

Chapter Fourteen

S kye placed the utensils down on the table next to every place setting. She was a nervous wreck and she truly wasn't sure if she was coming or going. Today was the day Betty was coming over to the house to meet up with Skye and see Lula. They had decided it would be best for Betty to pay a few visits to Lula so that they could get re-acquainted before she assumed custody of her. That way Lula wouldn't be overwhelmed with leaving Skye to go back with Betty. Skye had been praying that Lula would remember her birth mother. She wanted the entire process to be as easy as possible for the sweet girl. Her own feelings weren't nearly as important. She was quickly learning that a mother always put her child first.

She had decided on a cute hunter green cordu-roy dress with a pair of ballet flats. What did a person wear when they were meeting their fos-ter daughter's birth mother? It was silly of her to make a big deal out of her outfit, but there wasn't much in this situation she could control. She might as well distract herself with the contents of her wardrobe.

Betty had requested Ryan's presence at this meeting, which suited Skye just fine. He was an incredible source of strength and inspiration. Together they had decided to sit down for a meal with Betty so they could all get to know one another better. Gracelyn was also going to be present for moral support.

Ryan walked into the dining room carrying a vase filled with white roses from a local florist. He placed them on the sideboard table. "These are for you. I hope they make today a little bit brighter."

"That's sweet of you," she said, dipping her head down so she could sniff the exquisite flowers. "I'm still a little nervous. I'm not sure that I know how to pretend as if this is just another Saturday afternoon."

"You don't have to put on an act for anyone. Meeting with Betty isn't going to be adversarial. This is about bridging the gap and doing what's in Lula's best interest."

"Thanks for the reminder," she said. "And for being here for me and Lula," she added. "Throughout this entire journey she's always been what matters most of all."

At the sound of her name, Lula let out a gurgle

and began saying her favorite word, *Bye*. Skye and Ryan chuckled at the expression on the baby's face. With chubby cheeks and a guileless expression, she couldn't be any more adorable. Skye's breathing quickened at the idea of missing out on these sweet moments.

Be strong for Lula. Your love for her is stronger than your own hurts.

Just then Violet walked into the room carrying a basket of bread, which she placed in the center of the table. "I had to guard this bread with my life. Chase's mouth was watering."

Skye chuckled. Her nephew must be going through a growth spurt. Lately he had been eating second helpings at every meal. "I don't mind if he has a taste. After all, he's growing like Alaskan wild weed."

Violet grinned. "He really is. Pretty soon he's going to be taller than me."

Skye smiled at the mental image her sister's words brought to mind. Violet was five foot ten, so that was saying something.

The entire Drummond family would be present to meet Betty. After all, they had all been active and supportive of her fostering Lula. She wouldn't have been able to do it without their encouragement. And they all loved Lula just as much as Skye did. Chase had already shed tears over the news of Lula going back to be with her biological mother.

"How come she gets her back?" her nephew had asked, tears streaming down his face. "She didn't want her! And Lula's part of our family now."

Skye had soothed him by telling him, "Her mother loves her very much. Everyone deserves a second chance to get things right."

"But what if we don't ever see her again?" he'd asked.

Her nephew's question mirrored her own doubts. "Why don't we both pray that Lula is always part of our lives. How about that?"

Chase had bowed his head right then and there, offering up a heartfelt prayer that brought tears to her eyes. "Dear Lord, please keep Lula safe from all harm. Keep her happy and smiling. If You can, Lord, let us see Lula from time to time so she doesn't forget us. Amen."

Chase's prayer had centered her in a powerful way.

And now, they were all awaiting Betty's arrival with bated breath. Her father was so nervous he was pacing back and forth while occasionally peering out the window. Only Lula was oblivious to the implications of this meeting.

At twelve noon sharp, the doorbell rang. Skye answered the door with Lula sitting on her hip. She wanted Betty to see her daughter from the moment she stepped into the house. Skye had seen Betty around town at various town events, yet she was immediately struck by how young the teen looked. She thought there was a definite resemblance between her and Lula. Skye could tell she had dressed up today. She was wearing a long blue dress with a matching bow in her hair.

"Welcome, Betty. Gracelyn," Skye said, nodding to her older sister. Gracelyn was standing so close to Betty that they blended into one another. It was evident from her body language that Gracelyn was protective of her sister.

"Here. I brought these," Betty said, handing a tin to Skye. "They're brownies and blondies. My special recipe."

"Thank you," she said, taking the treat from Betty. She ushered them toward the living room. "I'd like you to meet my family. You already know Ryan."

Skye made the introductions and invited everyone to sit down and make themselves comfortable. She couldn't help but notice that Betty had been stealing glances at Lula ever since her arrival.

"Would you like to hold her?" Skye asked Betty, gesturing toward Lula.

"Yes, if I may," she said, sounding a bit nervous.

"Of course," Skye said, placing Lula in her arms.

Betty began to talk to the baby in a gentle

voice. "Hi there, Lula. Remember me? I haven't been around in a while but I want you to know that I think of you all the time. You're always in my prayers." Lula took a strand of Betty's hair and laced it through her fingers. Lula gazed at her with wide eyes, as if she knew this moment was important.

They played a game of peekaboo with Lula chortling with glee every time Betty opened up her hands and showed her face. Watching the two of them together caused the knot in Skye's stomach to ease up. This reunion was heartwarming and beautiful. Skye sensed that on some level Lula remembered Betty. That knowledge was comforting.

"She's gotten so big," Betty said, glancing over at Skye.

"She has," Skye agreed. "She's outgrown most of her clothes." Skye felt a pang as she thought of all the sweet little outfits she would never see Lula wear in the future.

"Why don't we sit down for lunch?" Abel suggested. "There'll be plenty of time to talk later."

Ryan grabbed hold of Skye's hand and held it tightly as they made their way toward the dining room. Although some of her nervousness had dissipated, her pulse was still racing. Ryan stuck close by, sitting down in the seat right next to her.

During lunch the discussion centered around the recent storm, various goings on in Serenity Peak and the fantastic choir concert. The subject of Lula wasn't broached at all. To Skye it seemed as if they were all tiptoeing around the very reason they had gathered today. As she cleared the table after lunch, Betty followed her into the kitchen.

"Can we talk privately, Skye? I think we need to get some things settled," Betty said in a soft voice. "I would like for Ryan to join us."

"Yes, that's a good idea," Skye said. "Why don't we talk in the den?"

She pulled Ryan to the side and clued him in as to what was happening. Skye then led the way to the small room her family used as a reading nook. It had been her mother's favorite place in the family home. She'd always called it her comfy cozy. Meeting in this particular room felt right to Skye.

"What about Gracelyn?" Ryan asked. "Do you want me to go get her?" He made a move toward the door.

"No," Betty answered, stopping him short. "We decided that I would do this part on my own. She's always done so much for me but I need to stand on my own two feet." She fiddled with a heart necklace hanging around her neck. Her hand was shaking.

Betty looked nervous and unsure of herself, despite Skye's best attempts to make her feel at ease. She wondered if she should have done something specific to reassure her about the situation.

"Betty, I want you to know that we understand you've been placed in a very difficult, high-pressure situation. We aren't judging you for any of the choices you've made," Skye told her. "We care about you very much."

"I appreciate you saying so, but I never thought you were judging me. You're both great people. That's why I dropped Lula off at your store." She smiled at Skye. "I studied your morning routine and I knew you would be at Sugar's Place at a certain time, like clockwork."

"Just knowing you picked me is so heart-warming," Skye said, reaching out and clasping Betty's hand in hers. "Fostering Lula has been an honor."

"I can see you love her a lot," Betty noted. In response, Skye nodded. She knew if she tried to speak the tears would be endless.

"So, where do we start? Tell us how you would like this to happen," Skye said. Although she was dreading hearing specifics about relinquishing Lula to Betty, it wasn't something she could avoid. Sticking her head in the sand wasn't going to accomplish anything.

"I've had a change of heart about Lula," Betty announced, looking back and forth between Skye and Ryan. "I've already discussed this with my sister."

Skye didn't dare speak. She wasn't sure if she had heard Betty correctly. Was this really happening?

"I'm not ready to be a mother. That's why I left her at Sugar's Place. I want to be ready, but I'm only seventeen years old. I'm trying my best to grow up." She wiped at her eyes and nose with her sleeve. "I love Lula a lot, but I'm just not ready to be a mom." Betty let out a sob. "I don't want you to think I'm a bad person or anything, but I really want Lula to have the best childhood. I don't think that I can give her that. Gracelyn loves her as well but she has an auto-immune disease that keeps flaring up. Helping me with the baby was an act of love, but it put a lot of stress on Gracelyn's body. I think this decision is the one I was always leaning toward."

Skye was struck by the emotion ringing out in Betty's voice. What an agonizing decision the teen had made.

"Betty, are you sure about this? Maybe you should take some time and think it over. This is a huge decision," Skye cautioned. "I don't want you to regret taking this step."

"I've thought of nothing else since the day

I found out that I was expecting her. And ever since that day it's gone around and around in my head." Tears slid down her cheeks and she brushed them away. "Gracelyn never wanted me to give Lula up in the first place. I think my wanting her back had a lot to do with trying to please her. And, in the end, what matters most is Lula. Not me. Not my feelings of shame. And not Gracelyn."

"Putting Lula first shows how much you love her, Betty," Ryan said. "A very mature decision, if you ask me."

Skye blinked away tears. Her emotions were all over the place. She was heartbroken for Betty and all the hard choices she'd had to make at such a tender age. At the same time, she was incredibly hopeful that she didn't have to say goodbye to Lula.

"Your decision is really brave, Betty," Skye said, stepping toward her so that there were only inches between them. On impulse she hugged the young woman, tightly wrapping her arms around her. She felt Betty hugging her back, and for a few moments, it seemed as if neither one wanted to let go. When they finally stepped away from one another, Skye noticed a sheen of tears in Betty's eyes.

"I know this isn't easy for you," Skye said. "And if there's anything I can do to make this whole process smoother, I'm here to help. Or if you ever just want a listening ear, I'm only a phone call away."

Betty smiled. "I'll definitely take you up on that."

"I'm going to hold you to it," Skye said.

"I want to officially relinquish Lula to you, Skye, if you still want to adopt her. Ryan mentioned it the other day," Betty said. "I would be honored and grateful to know you were raising her."

Skye looked over at Ryan, who had a sheepish expression etched on his face. "I'm sorry if I talked out of turn. I thought she should know."

"It's okay," she said. Everything was happening all at once and it felt both wonderful and a tad overwhelming. She had resigned herself to giving up Lula, and now, out of the blue, Betty was telling her she could adopt the daughter of her heart with her blessing. She almost wanted to pinch herself to make sure this was really happening.

"Are you all right?" Ryan asked, touching her arm in a comforting gesture.

"I'm fine," she said. "It's hard to put into words how I feel, because I know Betty's giving up a lot, while in return, I'm getting so much. Basically everything that I wanted."

"You're worthy of being Lula's mother," Ryan

said. "That's what Betty's trying to tell you. And I second that thought."

"You love her just as much as I do," Betty said. "I know that. I watched you with her at the choir concert and at Humbled. I wasn't spying on you, but it was serendipitous that I was able to enjoy your interactions. I don't have a single doubt about you adopting her. And for what it's worth, I'll provide a statement of support if that will help."

Tears of gratitude slid down Skye's cheeks. Despite her age, Betty was such a wise young woman with a heart as big as the Alaskan tundra. "Oh, that would be wonderful. And you will always have access to Lula. And there will always be a place for you at our table."

"Just what I wanted to hear," Betty said. "I have to warn you, Gracelyn is having a hard time accepting this and she hasn't fully warmed up to the idea. She might be a little prickly."

"She's probably just being a protective older sister," Ryan said.

"I have one of those, so I totally understand," Skye added. "We'll be gentle with her. And, of course, if you need more time to fully think things through, that's okay too." She wanted to show Betty as much grace as she could.

Betty shook her head. "I really don't. I had to drop out of high school when I was expecting Lula, so I'm planning to get my GED and do some other things. Maybe one day Lula will be proud of me."

"Without a doubt she will be," Skye said. And she meant it. She would tell Lula all about her birth mother's sacrifice, while ensuring that Betty had a forever role in Lula's life.

"Why don't we head back out there and join the others?" Ryan suggested. "I for one have been hankering for a taste of those brownies you brought."

As they left the room, Ryan threaded his hand through Skye's. She liked the solid feel of his hand in hers. For such a long time it had felt as if she couldn't lean on anyone, but now she couldn't imagine being without this wonderful man who had shown her nothing but devotion.

All of her prayers had suddenly been answered, even the ones she hadn't ever prayed for.

Chapter Fifteen

For the last few weeks, Skye had had a hard time believing she was truly on the path to adopting Lula. On several occasions she'd questioned her good fortune. Ryan understood her nervousness and the feeling that everything unfolding right now was too good to be true. Betty was steadfast in her desire to give Lula a strong foundation, one she knew she wasn't capable of providing herself. She hadn't wavered in her decision to support Skye's adoption filing when the time was right.

Finally, Skye was able to embrace the idea that God had brought Lula into her life so she could heal from past hurts.

With Skye beginning to accept the news, Ryan watched with delight as her confidence soared and strengthened. She was continuing with her certification and gathering information on the formal adoption process. Ryan supported her every step of the way, firm in the knowledge that Skye would be a fantastic mother.

At this point in time there was no indication that Skye would be facing an uphill battle in the adoption process, particularly with Betty's support. Ryan couldn't remember a time when he'd seen Skye so full of joy. It hummed and pulsed in the air around her. Their love was blossoming and everyone around Ryan told him he had never walked around with such assurance. All was right in his world due to Skye and a pint-sized charmer named Lula.

This evening was all about him and Skye. He had finally managed to plan a romantic date with the help of Uncle Judah. Although he loved Lula to bits, he needed this time just for the two of them. There was something important he needed to ask her. He had arranged for a private dining room at Northern Lights overlooking Kachemak Bay. They ate lobster and risotto by candlelight while romantic music played softly through a speaker. For dinner he'd arranged for her favorite dessert, chocolate mousse.

"This has been such a special treat for me," Skye gushed as the dessert plates were cleared and they walked over to the window to enjoy the view of the bay. "I've never had anyone do something this amazing for me."

"You deserve something fabulous after all you've been doing for others," Ryan said. She was a caretaker, but she also needed someone to make sure she was nurtured. He was happy to fill that role. Lately she had been packing lunches for him that he could take to work. Not your average sandwich, mind you. Cucumber and egg salad sandwiches on French bread. Tarragon chicken salad with cranberries and grapes on brioche bread. Swiss cheese and turkey on a croissant with pesto spread. He wasn't someone who tried new foods or read different types of books, but Skye was opening him up in so many ways.

"Did you see Abel's face when we announced that we're together?" Ryan asked, chuckling. "No one in your family seemed surprised, least of all Violet."

"My dad looked a bit smug if you ask me," Skye said. "As if he knew all along we were going to fall for one another."

"I seem to recall you not having such a great opinion of me a couple months ago," Ryan noted with a smirk. Each and every day he thanked the Lord she had changed her mind about him.

"Why, I have no idea what you're talking about," Skye demurred, batting her lashes. "I always thought you were the bee's knees."

Ryan wrapped his arms around her waist and pulled her against his chest. "Have I told you lately that I'm one fortunate man?"

Skye looked up at him with an expression

that radiated pure contentment. "Have I told you lately that you make me very happy?"

It was time. As far as he was concerned, there couldn't be a better moment to lay it all on the line. He knew with a deep certainty that he wanted to walk through life with this woman. His other half. His soul mate.

"That's all I ever want to do, Skye. If given the opportunity, I'd like to do it for a lifetime."

Skye's beautiful baby blues widened.

"I know this might seem kind of fast." He wiped his brow with the back of his hand. Why was he breaking out in a sweat in the winter? His nerves were shot. So much was riding on Skye's answer to this monumental question. He knew he wanted this more than anything else, but would she feel the same way?

"You mean the world to me. You're my everything," he said. "I think there's always been a part of me that's loved you, even when I knew that I couldn't. Or shouldn't." He reached for Skye's hand and got down on bended knee. He heard Skye let out a little gasp. "Skye Drummond. I've never known anyone as worthy of a happily-ever-after as you. And it would be the honor of my life to be your husband." He reached into his jacket pocket and pulled out a cedar box. When he looked up at Skye there were tears streaming down her face. He propped the box open, revealing a stunning antique diamond ring. It flashed and sparkled from its throne, brilliant and beautiful.

"Will you be my wife? I ask you this question knowing that you've been disappointed before by someone you wanted to make a life with. I want you for a lifetime, Skye. I don't have a single doubt that you're my forever. And I promise to never lose sight of that."

Skye's hands were covering most of her face and her breathing was a bit choppy.

"Is that a yes? A maybe?" Ryan asked, doubt coursing through him at her silence. She hadn't uttered a single word.

"It's one hundred percent, absolutely, positively a yes," Skye said in a trembling voice. "We've known each other all of our lives, so it may seem fast to some, but this moment has been in the making for a lifetime." She held out her hand. "I would be honored to wear your ring."

Ryan's chest tightened as he gently slid the diamond on her finger. "This was my great-granny's ring. She left it to me when she passed away."

Skye looked down at it. "Oh, Ryan. That makes it even more special. It's a legacy ring."

Moisture pooled in his eyes. He got to his feet. "She was a wonderful woman. Nothing was more important to her than faith and family. Her family didn't want her to marry my great-granddad but she followed her heart. They were married for sixty-six years and they never spent a single night apart."

She smiled. "They were true to their vows. Jeb and Emmaline."

"That's the kind of man I aim to be. A man of faith and a vow keeper."

"You're such an outstanding man, Ryan. Clearly, you take after Jeb," she said, grinning broadly. "It's in your DNA."

He looked down for a moment. There was so much pressing on his heart he wasn't sure he could express all his emotions. "My mother bailed on her marriage to my father and I've tried really hard not to judge her. I know that marriage is tough, but I've also learned from watching my parents' mistakes." He dipped his head down and pressed a kiss on her temple. "I'll never give up on us, no matter how hard life may get down the road."

"Neither will I, Ryan," Skye promised. "I know now that everything in life happens for a reason. Weeping may endure for a night, but joy cometh in the morning."

The passage from Psalm 30 had always been one of Ryan's personal favorites. Despite the pain and anguish life sometimes brought, the sun continued to shine. Hope was ever present. He and Skye were living proof that the past didn't determine one's future. Holding on to hope had served them both well and led them to their very own happily-ever-after.

Epilogue

Ryan hoisted his daughter up in the air as her tinkling laughter rang out in the stillness of an Alaskan afternoon. Lula's little pink hat bobbed as she flew a few feet.

"Not so high," Skye cautioned. "She just had lunch."

Ryan easily caught Lula on her way down and flashed his wife a playful grin. "Mama isn't happy with me, Lula. She thinks I might drop you."

"Mama," Lula said, pointing a chubby finger at Skye.

"Yes, I'm your Mama," Skye said, her chest bursting with joy at hearing her daughter calling her Mama. Never in a million years had she imagined such an incredible occurrence. Lula was now officially their adopted daughter—Lula Campbell. Skye thought her name had a certain ring to it.

"We should head inside," Ryan suggested, looking at his watch.

"You're right. Betty should be arriving any moment now," Skye said excitedly.

They went inside the house where the heady smell of chocolate chip cookies wafted in the air. Skye had made a batch for Betty to take home with her after their visit. They had established a friendship with Betty that was built on open communication and mutual respect. As promised, she was always welcome at their home.

A few minutes later a knock sounded on the front door, announcing Betty's arrival. When they opened the door she was standing on the doorstep with an oversize teddy bear in her hands. Lula didn't hesitate to tug at the teddy bear and tried to pull it down to her level.

"She's getting so big," Betty gushed. "I can hardly believe it."

Ryan made a face. "We know! She's eating us out of house and home."

Skye playfully swatted him. "That's not true. She's a growing, healthy girl. Here, I have some photos for you to keep." She handed Betty a thick envelope. Skye never let a day go by without taking pics of her little girl. She knew Betty appreciated the photos and the stories that went along with them.

"Why, thank you," Betty said, clutching the packet to her chest. "I can't wait to look at these later. Gracelyn told me she was here a few days ago."

"Yes," Skye said, grinning. "Auntie G visited us and spent a lot of time with Lula. We always want her to feel at home here and to maintain a relationship with her niece."

"Thanks. It's important to me that she's part of the circle of love for Lula."

"Mine," Lula said, reaching again for the teddy bear.

They all chuckled, including Lula, who was grinning from ear to ear as Betty gave her the stuffed animal.

"We recognize what a huge sacrifice you made in putting Lula up for adoption," Skye said, reaching out and squeezing Betty's hand.

"It was the right decision," Betty said. "Being able to see her regularly is such a blessing. And I'm grateful she has two such loving parents."

"That's the beauty of an open adoption," Ryan said. "The bond between you and Lula will never be severed." He handed Lula over to Betty, who nuzzled her face against Lula's neck.

"Oh, you smell like baby powder and sweetness," Betty said. "And everything wonderful."

"Not all the time," Ryan teased. "I've changed some stinky diapers."

Betty giggled while Skye shook her head at her husband's never-ending baby jokes.

She was proud to call Ryan her husband. Their wedding had been an intimate service at Serenity Church, followed by a reception at Sugar Works. Her sister had been her maid of honor while Ryan's friend Brody had served as the best man. This time around, Skye had known with a deep certainty that her groom would be meeting her at the altar ready to pledge forever to her. And when she recited her vows to Ryan, she had been firm in the knowledge that they would be united for a lifetime.

They sat down to dinner and caught up on what was going on in their lives. Betty was working on getting her GED with the hopes of going to college next year. They filled Betty in on all of Lula's milestones—new words, first steps, favorite foods and toys.

When it was time for Lula to be put down for the night, Skye suggested that Betty have the task of tucking her in.

"Are you sure it's all right?" Betty asked with wide eyes.

"Why wouldn't it be? She adores you," Skye reassured her.

"I just figured she would expect her parents to do the honors."

"Lula knows you, Betty. And she loves you. Trust me, she'll go to sleep for you," Skye said, making a shooing motion in the direction of Lula's nursery.

"You've got this," Ryan said, cheering her on with enthusiasm.

Betty gently took Lula by the hand and walked her toward her bedroom after Ryan and Skye gave her good-night kisses. Twenty minutes later Betty emerged from the bedroom, looking content. "She went down right away but I just sat there for a bit and stared at her while she slept. I still can't believe I created something so wonderful."

"And we'll always be grateful you did," Ryan said.

As they said their good-nights to Betty they made plans to meet up with her in a few weeks for an outing at the Serenity Falls. They wanted to incorporate the young woman into their life so that Lula would always know her birth mother.

All felt right in their world as Skye and Ryan sat in the living room holding hands and marveling at the turn of events in their lives.

"I can't believe that this is us," Skye said with a shake of her head. Her voice was thick with emotion.

"I know what you mean," Ryan said, leaning over and placing a tender kiss on his wife's lips. "This is all I've ever wanted wrapped up in a nice big bow. I won't ever need anything more than this," Ryan murmured.

"What if our family was blessed with another member? A pint-sized one?" Skye asked, a smile twitching at her lips.

Ryan let out a surprised sound. "Are you? Are we…?" he asked, stammering.

She bobbed her head. "We are!"

Ryan jumped up and let out a whoop of excitement.

"Shh. You'll wake up Lula," Skye said, laughing at his enthusiasm.

"Sorry, sweetheart," he apologized in a hushed tone. "I'm so over-the-moon happy. This all just seems too good to be true." He pulled Skye to a standing position and began dancing with her, gracefully twirling her around. She placed her arms around his neck and leaned into him.

"How's this for a happy-ever-after?" she asked, standing on tiptoes so she could brush her lips over his.

"It's way more perfect than I ever imagined," Ryan said, pulling her against his chest and placing his arms around her waist. "Life is so sweet. May we always be as happy as we are right now," he whispered in her ear.

"We will be," Skye said. "I promise."

* * * * *

If you enjoyed
An Alaskan Blessing

Don't miss
Her Alaskan Return
by Belle Calhoune!

Available now from Love Inspired.

Discover more at LoveInspired.com

Dear Reader,

Welcome back to Serenity Peak, Alaska. I hope you enjoyed Skye and Ryan's love story. This book deals with a heroine who suffers from feelings of unworthiness. With the support of the hero, her family and her faith, Skye emerges as a stronger person by the end of the story. Finding love with someone she can implicitly trust is all she's ever wanted. We go through challenging circumstances in life, some that bring us to our knees. Feelings of shame are hard to navigate, but when those emotions aren't dealt with, they can totally derail a person's life.

Skye and Ryan are both characters who manage to rise above their pasts and forge a path forward. Each of them has relied on their faith as an anchor as they weather difficult times in their lives. Although Skye rescues Lula, in a sense the sweet baby saves Skye by showing her that she still has the capacity to love.

I'm honored to be writing for the Love Inspired line. Being able to work at home in my pajamas is a huge perk. You can find me online at my Author Belle Calhoune Facebook page or join my newsletter at bellecalhoune.com. Until next time!

Blessings,
Belle